TO KN
IS TO FEAR HER!

Like a dark angel of the night she strikes! Sleek, elegant, beautiful—and deadly! Follow Marvel's latest and greatest sensation as she takes on:

The Hordes of Hydra!
The Brothers Grimm!
The Hangman!
Werewolf by Night!
The Man Who Couldn't Die!
And more!

MARVEL TRIUMPHS AGAIN!

This volume contains the complete
Spider-Woman epics originally presented in
Marvel Spotlight #32 and Spider-Woman #1-8.

Production Supervised by
Sol Brodsky

Production Co-ordination by
Irene Vartanoff

Cover Art by
Joe Sinnott

Cover and Interior Production,
Type, Art and Color by
Carl Gafford
Sharon Ing
Paty
Carl Wirshba
Andy Yanchus

With an Editorial Assist by
Danny Fingeroth

Inspiration by
Stan Lee

STAN LEE
presents

TM

PUBLISHED BY POCKET BOOKS NEW YORK

POCKET BOOKS, a Simon & Schuster division of
GULF & WESTERN CORPORATION
1230 Avenue of the Americas, New York, N.Y. 10020

Published by arrangement with Marvel Comics Group

ISBN: 0-671-83026-0

First Pocket Books printing September, 1979

10 9 8 7 6 5 4 3 2 1

Printed in the U.S.A.

STAN LEE PRESENTS: SPIDER-WOMAN!™

ARCHIE GOODWIN WRITER/EDITOR * SAL BUSCEMA & JIM MOONEY ILLUSTRATORS * IRV WATANABE, LETTERER JANICE COHEN, COLORIST

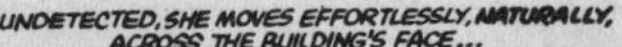

YET EVEN THEN, SHE WAITS...

NOT THAT ANYTHING COULD PREVENT MY DOING WHAT I MUST TONIGHT!

WHILE OVERHEAD, PROTECTED BY CLOUDS AND ANTI-RADAR FORCE SCREENS...

HAIL HYDRA INDEED, ALPHA LEADER...
GLORY IS ALMOST OURS!
I HARDLY DARE BELIEVE IT, COMMANDER!
THAT OUR ISOLATED RESERVE UNIT MIGHT ACCOMPLISH WHAT A SUCCESSION OF SUPREME HYDRAS COULD NOT...
WE SHALL, YOU DOUBTING FOOL! MY ASSASSINATION SCHEME GOES PRECISELY AS PLANNED!
SOON THAT HATED FACE I KEEP BEFORE ME ON THE ALTERNATE VIEWSCREEN...

...WILL BELONG TO A DEAD MAN! NEVER AGAIN WILL HYDRA'S DREAM OF WORLD CONQUEST BE THWARTED BY...
NICK FURY, DIRECTOR OF S.H.I.E.L.D.!
BUT BEFORE THAT HAPPENS...

...COL. FURY IS DUE FOR SOME OTHER LUMPS!
WOK!
YOU WANT TO ASK QUESTIONS, FURY? THIS IS MY ONLY ANSWER!

BACK OFF, PRISONER! ANY ESCAPE ATTEMPT WILL ONLY GET YOU BLASTED TO--
BITE YOUR LIP, JUNIOR! THIS BIRD'S LIVIN' PROOF THAT THERE'S A NEST OF HYDRA VIPERS AROUND WE AIN'T EVER DISCOVERED!
WHY ELSE D'YA THINK I CAME HUSTLIN' HERE FROM MAIN H.Q.?

EVEN IF SHIELD DID SHOOT PRISONERS-- WHICH IT DON'T--HE KNOWS WE WOULDN'T HARM OUR ONLY LEAD!
SO BUTT OUT AN' LEMME PLAY THIS HIS WAY.
FINE, COLONEL--
--IF RIDING A DESK HASN'T RUINED YOU AS ANY SORT OF A CHALLENGE!

OH, I AIN'T IN THE CLASS OF A BIG-DEAL HYDRA HUNTER-ELITE LIKE YOU, GOLDILOCKS--
WUNNGH!
KRAK!
--BUT IN MY OWN FEEBLE WAY, I TRY!!

AND IN A CORRIDOR ON THE SAME FLOOR...
...SOMEONE ELSE IS TRYING...AND SUCCEEDING!
I'M CLOSE! MUST BE MORE CAREFUL THAN EVER.
CAN'T LET ANGER--OR CONCERN--CAUSE ME TO MAKE A MISTAKE!

SCUTTLING STEALTHILY, ARACHNE, THE GIRL WITH THE SPIDER-POWERS, MOVES TOWARD THE ROOM SHE SEEKS...
SOUNDS LIKE THE INTERROGATION IS GETTING ROUGH!
THINK COL. FURY WILL NEED US IN THERE?
OUR FIRE-BREATHIN' RAMROD? NOT LIKELY! BESIDES--
RROGATION
ROOM

--YOU HAVE OTHER THINGS TO WORRY ABOUT!
WOM
SPLAK

THE FALLEN GUARDS DO NOT RISE... AND THEIR ATTACKER LEAPS FOR THE INTERROGATION ROOM'S STEEL DOOR!
BA-DOM!
COL. FURY! WE'VE GOT A VISITOR... DEFINITELY UNFRIENDLY!
STOP 'EM OR STALL 'EM--
--WHILE I PUT THE FINISHING TOUCHES ON HYDRA'S LITTLE HOTSHOT!
KA-RAK

ENOUGH! FOR WHAT YOU'VE DONE TO HIM--
--YOU'LL ANSWER TO ME!
HER VOICE IS SOFT BUT EDGED WITH RAGE. DEFTLY DELIBERATELY, THE SPIDER-WOMAN BEGINS TO REMOVE A GLOVE...

WE SAW WHAT YOU DID TO THAT DOOR, LADY... AND WE'RE IMPRESSED!
SO BACK OFF FAST... OR WE'LL BE FORCED TO USE ALL THIS ARTILLERY WE CARRY!
NO...
...NONE OF YOU WILL HAVE THE CHANCE! NOT ONCE YOU FEEL MY VENOM BOLTS!
FORTUNATELY FOR YOU, THEY'RE NOT FATAL AT THIS RANGE.
ZDAK
WHAT TH--?! EVERY BLASTED MAN... TOTALLED!
AND YOU'RE NEXT! BUT THE BOLT WILL COME WHEN I'M TOUCHING YOU.
BRINGING DEATH FOR WHAT YOU'VE DONE...
...TO THE MAN I LOVE!

SILENCE FILLS THE CHAMBER... AS THE LADY CALLED ARACHNE STALKS FORWARD...
...TOWARD THE MOMENT SHE'S BEEN GUIDED TO SINCE ONE FATEFUL DAY IN A SMALL ALPINE VILLAGE...

WITCH! AGENT OF SATAN!
FLEE... OR DIE!
WHY ARE YOU DOING THIS... WHAT HAVE I DONE?!
I--I CAN'T REMEMBER... I CAN'T!!

BUT SHE COULD REACT...
...USING HER STRANGE POWERS...
ZDAK!
...TO REACH THE ROAD...

...WHERE AN APPROACHING LIMOUSINE STOPPED.
STAY YOUR HAND, CHILD!
I HAVE HEARD OF YOU AND YOUR NOVEL... ABILITIES. I CAME HERE TO HELP.
HE WAS COUNT OTTO VERMIS...AN AREA COMMANDER...

...FOR THE ORGANIZATION KNOWN AS HYDRA.
A NAME TO STRIKE TERROR...IF ONE HAD MEMORY OF THEIR PAST DEEDS. THE FUGITIVE GIRL DID NOT.
SHE KNEW HER NAME. HER MEMORIES COULD BE COUNTED IN DAYS. ALL ELSE WAS VOID. A VOID ABOUT TO BE FILLED... WITH LIES.
...THUS, YOU SEE, WE TOO HAVE BEEN UNFAIRLY PERSECUTED...
HAIL HYDRA!
...MADE OUTLAWS BY AN UNCOMPREHENDING WORLD WE STRUGGLE SOLELY TO AID AND IMPROVE.
CAN YOU SYMPATHIZE WITH OUR CAUSE, CHILD...CAN YOU JOIN OUR FIGHT?
SHE DID...

...FINDING COMFORT IN THE HYDRA COMMANDER'S STERN, ALMOST FATHERLY TREATMENT...
...AND HIS PROMISES TO PENETRATE THAT DARK BARRIER CLOUDING HER MEMORY.
YOU WILL MERELY HAVE A PLEASANT, DREAMLESS SLEEP, ARACHNE...
...THE REST IS UP TO THE MIND PROBE.

AND WHEN ITS WORK WAS FINISHED...
LORD! NO WONDER THE PAST HAS BEEN TRAUMATIZED FROM HER MIND!
HER CREATION... THAT INCIDENT...! I-IT'S--
IT'S PERFECT, DOCTOR.
FAR BETTER THAN I'D HOPED. I CAN USE IT ALL...
...MOLD HER INTO HYDRA'S DEADLIEST WEAPON EVER!

SHE WAS TOLD THE MIND PROBE WAS UNSUCCESSFUL...
ZADT!
...THEN BEGAN TRAINING UNDER THE UNIT'S TOP COMBAT AGENT...

...UNTIL HER NATURAL POWERS WERE HONED TO FIGHTING PERFECTION.
SHE WAS GIVEN A COSTUME, DESIGNED TO CHANNEL AND CONTROL THOSE POWERS, AND... SPIDER-WOMAN WAS BORN!

AND SOON... KNEW LOVE.
IT HAD TO BE, ARACHNE. ALL THIS TIME WORKING SO CLOSELY...
YES, JARED...
OH, YES!

BUT TO KNOW LOVE IS TO BE VULNERABLE...TO HURT, TO FEAR...TO RAGE!
JARED CAPTURED BY SHIELD? IF THEY'VE HARMED HIM--
THEIR DIRECTOR IS A FANATIC WHEN IT COMES TO HYDRA...
VWOM!
...YOU KNOW THAT. YOU KNOW NONE OF US CAN EVER BE SAFE UNTIL--

"--NICK FURY DIES!" THE WORDS SCREAM IN ARACHNE'S MIND, DEMANDING ACTION...

NOT WHILE I GOT A MOVE OR TWO LEFT, PEOPLE!
YAHHH!
ZA-DAK!
N-NO!

JARED! I DIDN'T MEAN--
YOU BOTH BLEW IT! THIS ALARM'LL BRING--
I...
WAP

WUNK!
NOTHING--!
NOTHING THAT CAN COME IN TIME TO SAVE YOU, NICK FURY!
THE SHIELD DIRECTOR'S HEAD SLAMS HARD INTO DIALS AND LEVERS...

...TOGGLES AND SWITCHES, TRIGGERING ACTION ON THE ELABORATE CONSOLE...
...AND, A REVELATION!
W-WHAT...?

THE VIDEO-PLAYBACK SCREEN IS SUDDENLY ALIVE WITH SCENES OF TERRORISM AND BRUTALITY...
AND IN THEIR CENTER...
JARED! IT... CAN'T BE YOU! IT'S SOME SORT OF FAKERY...

...OR ELSE EVERYTHING I'VE BEEN TOLD HAS BEEN A LIE!
AND HYDRA HAS MANIPULATED ME... USED ME...!
IT'S...ONE OF THEIR... SPECIALTIES, LADY...

THE GIRL'S REACTION IS SWIFT... TEARS ARE REPLACED BY COLD ANGER...ANGER FOR...

BUT NEITHER FURY NOR APPROACHING GUARDS CAN HALT THE SPIDER-WOMAN...

THE EXPLOSION FADES, BUT FLAME, CHAOS, AND CONFUSION REMAIN TO FILL ITS WAKE...

THE GLIDING ATTACK SENDS THE HYDRA RANKS SCATTERING...

THE LITTLE WITCH IS TOTALLY BERSERK!
MY MEN WILL REGROUP TO FIGHT HER... BUT UNTIL THEN, I'D BEST USE THE EMERGENCY ESCAPE SYSTEM!
AND COUNT VERMIS RACES ON...

...INTO THE MONASTERY'S DEEPEST VAULTS.
GOOD! SHE'S NOT EVEN CLOSE YET.
ONCE BEYOND THE GATE, I'LL BE--

THOM!
CAUGHT!
YOU AND JARED TAUGHT ME HOW TO MOVE SWIFTLY THROUGH A BUILDING'S VENTILATION SYSTEM, REMEMBER?!

NOW! YOU HAVE SOME THINGS TO TELL ME...
W-WAIT...! THOSE SOUNDS FROM UPSTAIRS!
GUNS...! MORE BLASTS...! ALMOST AS IF--

A FULL-SCALE ATTACK IS UNDERWAY...LED BY NICK FURY OF SHIELD!
POUR IT ON 'EM!
WE GOT A BREAK... LET'S NOT BOOT IT!
FZAK!
BDUM

YOU LET THEM FOLLOW OUR FLYER! VERY WELL, A BARGAIN THEN...
YOU MIGHT FORCE WHAT YOU WANT FROM ME, ARACHNE...OR I MIGHT RESIST AND DIE WITH YOUR SECRET...
BUT IF I WERE ALLOWED TO FLEE AND AVOID CAPTURE BY SHIELD...

THE GIRL STUDIES VERMIS FOR A MOMENT, THEN...NODS.
VERY WISE, CHILD... KNOWING WHEN TO BARTER! NOW, A FEW STEPS THIS WAY...

...AND OUR GOAL APPEARS BEFORE US!
YOUR GOAL...NOT MINE.

TRUE, MY DEAR! AND PERHAPS JUST AS WELL...SINCE THIS ROCKET PLANE WAS DESIGNED TO CARRY ONLY ONE PASSENGER.
AND THE HYDRA COMMANDER MOVES SWIFTLY, EAGERLY, FOR THE LADDER TO THE ESCAPE CRAFT'S COCKPIT...

BARGAINS ARE TWO-SIDED, COUNT! YOU GO NOWHERE...UNTIL I KNOW THE FULL STORY OF MY ORIGIN!
NEVER FEAR, ARACHNE... YOU WON'T BE CHEATED OF THAT.
OF YOUR TRUE BIRTH... I KNOW NOTHING.
BUT I CAN TELL YOU MUCH OF THE MOMENT WHEN THE EXPLODING ENERGY WAS UNLEASHED...

"...THAT SHAPED YOU INTO WHAT YOU ARE NOW!

"THE SHAPER WAS THE HIGH EVOLUTIONARY...*HIS INSTRUMENT, THE GENETIC ACCELERATOR...
SUCCESS...AS ALWAYS! UNCOUNTABLE EONS OF EVOLUTION...ACHIEVED IN MERE MOMENTS.
BUT THIS SUCCESS IS UNIQUE COMPARED TO MY OTHERS.
IN THE PAST, I HAVE WROUGHT "NEW MEN" FROM VARIOUS ANIMAL SPECIALS...
*THIS IS BEFORE H.E.'S HISTORIC DEBUT IN THE MIGHTY THOR #134 --ARCH.

...BUT YOU ARE MY FIRST FEMALE AND I AM PLEASED...
I LABORED FAR LONGER AT YOUR CREATION...MADE FAR GREATER GENETIC IMPROVEMENTS...SO YOU WOULD BE FAR NEARER HUMAN...
...THOUGH DESCENDED FROM A TOTALLY DIFFERENT SPECIES!

"DIFFERENT SPECIES?!" B-BUT...WITH THE SPIDER LIKE POWERS I POSSESS THAT COULD ONLY MEAN...
HE HAD A MOST FITTING REASON--
--FOR NAMING YOU "ARACHNE!"

NO! YOU'RE LYING...IF SUCH A THING WERE TRUE ...I'D KNOW IT!
NOT IF IT WERE TRAUMATIZED FROM YOUR MEMORY!

BUT, LEARN FOR YOURSELF, CHILD! THE STORY IS FAR FROM OVER...
...YOUR PAIN HAS BARELY BEGUN.

"THE HIGH EVOLUTIONARY WAS A PROUD FATHER TO YOU, BUT HIS NEW MEN--THE KNIGHTS WITH WHICH HE WAS BUILDING A MODERN DAY CAMELOT--WERE FAR LESS THAN BROTHERS.
"THEIR ANIMAL NATURES MADE THEM SENSE YOUR DIFFERENCE...
"THEY WERE REPELLED...
"...YOU WERE OSTRACIZED.

"IT WAS AN INSTINCTIVE REACTION THAT COULD NOT BE OVERCOME. AND, IN TIME, IT DROVE YOU TO FLIGHT...

"BUT THE SUDDEN NOISE CAUSED YOU TO REACT! INSTINCTIVELY...
"IRRATIONALLY...
ZADT!
"FATALLY."

...A BODY WHICH CAN MANUFACTURE ITS OWN VENOM MAY NO DOUBT BE IMMUNE TO OTHER POISONS!

ENJOY THIS INTRO TO SPIDER-WOMAN, EFFENDI? WELL, SO DID MARVELDOM ASSEMBLED! THEY DEMANDED MORE... AND THEY GOT IT. SO READ ON--THE EXCITEMENT CONTINUES IN:

THE REAL ORIGIN OF SPIDER-WOMAN!

Stan Lee PRESENTS: THE MYSTERIOUS SPIDER-WOMAN!

YOU THINK YOU'VE READ IT ALL WHEN IT COMES TO SUPER-HEROINES? GUESS AGAIN, MARVELITE.

MARV WOLFMAN WRITER / EDITOR · CARMINE INFANTINO PENCILS · TONY DEZUNIGA INKS · JOE ROSEN LETTERS · GLYNIS WEIN COLORS · ARCHIE GOODWIN CREATOR / CONSULTING ED.

BUT, HAVE I ANY OTHER CHOICE?
I'VE NO JOB, NO HOPE FOR FINDING ONE.

MY PAST LIFE'S BEEN A SHAMBLES-- WHAT I WAS, WHO I AM, HOW I GOT THESE BIZARRE POWERS-- I'VE TOO DAMN MANY QUESTIONS...
...AND TOO DAMN FEW ANSWERS.
BUT, I'M HUNGRY... HAVEN'T EATEN FOR DAYS. SO NOW I'M FORCED TO BECOME A--
IOTA'S
TOMA

NO!
MAYBE MY PAST'S BEEN DESTROYED, BUT I WON'T RUIN MY FUTURE AS WELL.
KLANG!

WHATEVER I MAY HAVE BEEN MEANS NOTHING NOW. I WON'T STEAL... NOT EVEN TO LIV--
NO! FOOTSTEPS COMING THIS WAY.
THANK HEAVEN FOR MY EXTRA-ACUTE HEARING. ANOTHER SECOND AND I WOULD HAVE BEEN SPOTTED.

EH? AIN'T NO ONE 'ERE? BUT--
AHHH, IT'S JUST ME NERVES AGAIN. PROBABLY S'MORE RATS KNOCKING OVER THE CANS.

YEAH, JUST S'MORE RATS. BETTER GET OUT THE TRAPS AGAIN AN' SET 'EM.

'SIDES, ARCHIE, D'YA REALLY WANT TA SEE IF THERE'S ANYTHIN' ELSE IN THERE?
YOU'RE TOO BLASTED OLD TO GET INVOLVED WITH REAL TROUBLE. ISN'T THAT WHAT FLORRIE ALWAYS SAYS--? "TOO BLASTED OLD FOR MUCH A' ANYTHIN'!"
SO GET ON YOUR WAY, ARCHIE. CHECK OUT THE OTHER STORES ON YOUR ROUTE, AN' GET ON 'OME BEFORE IT'S TOO LATE.
YE OLD Shoppe

ARCHIE KALNAN'S FOOTSTEPS RECEDE AND FINALLY FADE...
ALMOST CAUGHT. PERHAPS I SHOULD HAVE BEEN.
SOMETIMES I THINK I SHOULD BE LOCKED AWAY WHERE I CAN'T HURT OTHERS...AND MORE--WHERE I CAN'T HURT MYSELF!
BLAST! SELF PITY? IS THERE ANY DEPTH I WON'T STOOP TO? I'M RESPONSIBLE FOR ALL MY ACTIONS. ME! NO ONE ELSE!

IF I DO SOMETHING WRONG, I'M THE ONLY ONE TO BLAME. NO ONE'S MANIPULATING MY LIFE ANYMORE. I'M FINALLY FREE.
SPANG
SO WHY IS EVERYTHING GOING WRONG FOR ME? WHY?

ALL RIGHT, CALM DOWN, GIRL-- CALM DOWN.
I KNOW I'M NOT A THIEF. I'VE TAKEN NOTHING, NO ONE WILL EVER KNOW I'VE BEEN HERE.
I CAN START ALL OVER AGAIN AND THIS TIME PLAN MY LIFE INSTEAD OF HAVING IT WORKED OUT FOR ME.
MY DAYS WITH THE HIGH EVOLUTIONARY ARE OVER. I'M FREE OF HYDRA'S CONTROL. I'M ON MY OWN-- FOR THE FIRST TIME IN MY LIFE!

HOLD IT!
WHO--?
THE MARKET'S CLOSED--! WHAT WERE YOU DOING IN THERE? AND WHY ARE YOU WEARING THAT COS--

I DIDN'T TAKE ANYTHING. I DIDN'T DO ANYTHING.
THAT'S NOT ANSWERING THE QUESTION, LADY. AND I'M SURE ANYONE AS GORGEOUS AS YOU MUST HAVE A READY ANSWER FOR THIS. DON'T YOU?

THERE'S NO WAY I CAN EXPLAIN MYSELF,
HEY!
AND NO ONE WOULD BELIEVE ME IF I COULD.
MY ONLY HOPE IS TO GET AWAY!

I'D SAY THAT WAS A CLEAR ADMISSION OF GUILT, BEAUTIFUL.
THAT MEANS I CAN'T LET YOU RUN OFF.

YOU CAN TRY STOPPING ME--
BTOK
OOOF
--BUT IT WON'T BE AS EASY AS YOU MAY THINK.

SO, YOU'RE STRONG, GORGEOUS. BUT THEN, SO AM I!
AND I STILL MEAN IT WHEN I SAY YOU'RE GOING NOWHERE!
BY THE WAY, MAYBE I SHOULD EXPLAIN MYSELF--I'M WORKING WITH SCOTLAND YARD, WHICH MEANS, SHORT AND SIMPLY--

--I'M TAKING YOU IN!
BUT FIRST--
RIPP
NO-- DON'T!
YOUR FACE! I-I'VE SEEN IT BEFORE!

YOU COULDN'T HAVE, AND YOU NEVER WILL AGAIN!
HEY, STOP!

NO GOOD, I REACTED TOO SLOWLY, AND THAT GAVE HER THE CHANCE TO RUN.
BUT, THAT FACE... THAT BEAUTIFUL FACE... I KNOW I'VE SEEN IT BEFORE.
BUT-- WHERE?

MORNING IN LONDON, A BRIGHT SUMMER'S DAY...
SEEMS TO MAKE NO DIFFERENCE HOW MUCH I TRY. THAT WAS ANOTHER TURN-DOWN FOR A JOB.
THAT'S AN EVEN DOZEN "SORRY, YOU WON'T DO'S" IN THREE DAYS.
WHAT'S WRONG WITH ME?
LOOK, IT'S HER AGAIN-- THE STRANGE ONE.
SHE MAKES ME QUEASY ALL OVER.

LOOK, IT'S THAT DREW LADY. MUM SAYS SHE'S REALLY WEIRD.
COR! AN' SHE SURE IS PRETTY.
I WONDER WHAT'S WRONG WITH HER?

THEY ALL SENSE IT. THEY KNOW I'M DIFFERENT.
SOMEHOW THEY REALIZE -- I'M NOT ALL HUMAN!
AND THAT MAKES ME EVEN MORE ALONE THAN I WAS BEFORE.

A FEW MINUTES LATER, IN A RAMSHACKLE LONDON TENEMENT...
OLLIE, THERE SHE IS AGAIN. GOD, SHE MAKES MY SKIN CRAWL.
WHY DID YOU INSIST ON RENTING HER THAT FLAT?

SHE SHOULD BE OUT IN THE GUTTER, OLLIE.
Y'KNOW, MRS. McGRUDER, SEVERAL OF THE WOMEN HERE ASKED ME THAT LATELY, AN' I'M TELLIN' YOU ALL THE SAME THING.
I SOMEHOW FEEL SORRY FOR THE LADY. Y'SEE, I SENSE SOMETHING TERRIBLY ALONE ABOUT HER...SOMETHING OUT OF PLACE.

HER EYES TELL ME SHE'S THE SUFFERING KIND, AND I JUST COULDN'T BEAR TO SEE THAT LOVELY FACE DO ANY MORE SUFFERING. NOT FOR A MEASLY FLAT.
AND THAT, MRS. McGRUDER, IS WHY I RENTED HER A ROOM, AND THAT IS WHY SHE WILL KEEP IT AS LONG AS SHE WANTS TO.
GOOD DAY NOW, I HAVE MY WORK TO DO.

THE DAY IS LONG AND ALONE, AND EVENTUALLY, NIGHT CALLS ONCE MORE...
WHAT AM I? WHERE DID I COME FROM?
WHO--WHO AM I?
DREAMS CLAIM THE YOUNG WOMAN. STRANGE NIGHT-MARES THAT SPEAK OF REALITY.

AND THERE ARE IMAGES... THE ONE CALLED MODRED THE MYSTIC...*
HE REACHED INTO HER MIND, AND HE LEARNED THE TRUTH.
*AS SHOWN IN MARVEL TWO-IN-ONE #33 --MARV.

HE LEARNED ALL THERE WAS ABOUT THIS WOMAN, AND HE PLAYED THE IMAGES FOR HER TO SEE.

THERE WAS THE PICTURE OF A MAN... A PICTURE THAT WENT BACK MANY YEARS... TO A SCIENTIFIC BREAKTHROUGH...*
I TELL YOU, MY GENETIC ACCELER-ATOR WORKS!
IMPOSSIBLE! RIDICU-LOUS! IT CAN NEVER WORK!
IT'S AN UGLY MOCKERY! NO MAN HAS THE RIGHT TO TAMPER WITH EVOLUTION!
*WAY BACK IN THOR #135.--MARV.

BUT THIS MAN DID, AND HE SOUGHT OUT HIS ONLY FRIENDS.
JOHN, YOU'RE THE ONLY ONE WHO BELIEVES ME... WHO TRUSTS ME.
AND YOU, MY FRIEND, BELIEVE IN ME!

YOU STUDY EVOLUTION, I STUDY ARACHNIDS. IN A WAY, OUR SCIENCES ARE RELATED.
ARTHROPODS LIVED BEFORE MAN, THEY'LL CONTINUE TO THRIVE LONG AFTER WE'RE GONE!
THEY'VE SURVIVED THE ICE AGE, RADIATION, POLLUTION!

IF WE COULD SOMEHOW INFUSE MAN WITH THE SPECIAL PROPERTIES OF SPIDERS, THEN MAN COULD ADAPT... COULD EVOLVE INTO A BEING CAPABLE OF LIVING IN TOMORROW'S WORLD OF OVER-POLLUTION AND RADIATION.
MAN COULD SURVIVE THE TOTAL GAMUT OF OUR TECHNOLOGICAL DEVASTATION.

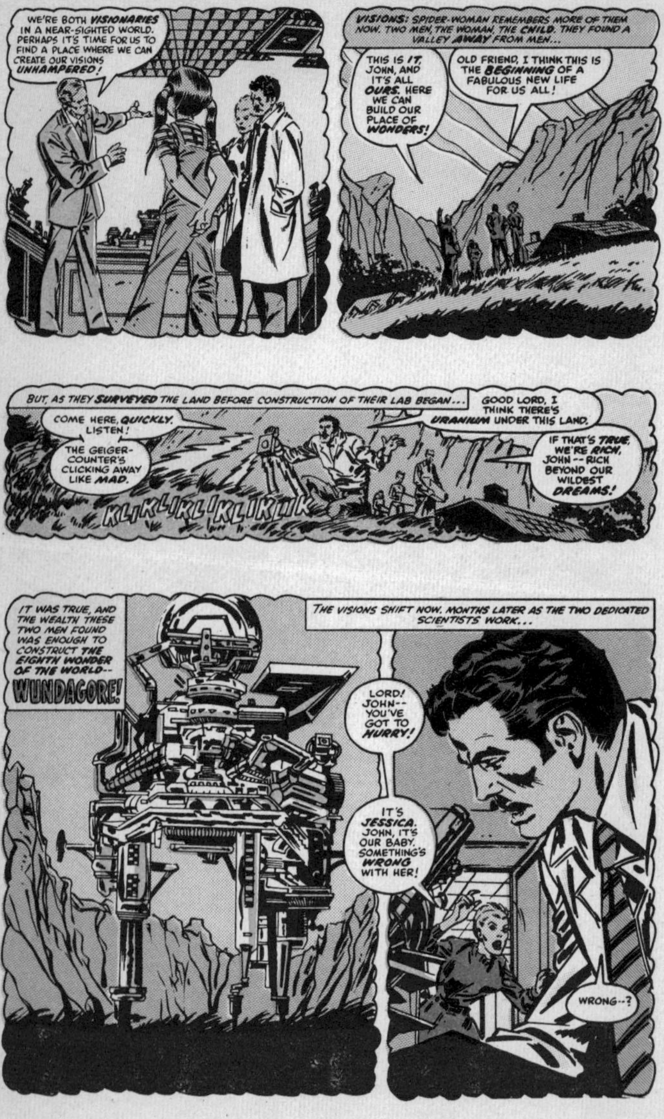

IT WAS TRUE, AND THE WEALTH THESE TWO MEN FOUND WAS ENOUGH TO CONSTRUCT THE EIGHTH WONDER OF THE WORLD--

WUNDAGORE!

THE VISIONS SHIFT NOW. MONTHS LATER AS THE TWO DEDICATED SCIENTISTS WORK...

LORD! JOHN-- YOU'VE GOT TO HURRY!

IT'S JESSICA. JOHN, IT'S OUR BABY. SOMETHING'S WRONG WITH HER!

WRONG--?

IT'S RADIATION... FROM THE URANIUM. SHE'S SICK, JOHN... DEATHLY SICK!
YOU'VE GOT TO COME!
I-I NEVER THOUGHT THE URANIUM WOULD AFFECT JESSIE. MY GOD, IF ANYTHING HAPPENS TO HER--

HOW IS SHE? TELL ME!
SHE'S GOT IT BAD, JOHN. THE RADIATION POISONING MUST HAVE BEEN BUILDING FOR MONTHS.
I PLACED HER IN MY CRYOGENIC UNIT* TO SLOW DOWN THE RATE OF HER CELL DESTRUCTION.
*A FREEZING UNIT USED IN MEDICINE -- MARV.

BUT THERE'S NOTHING I-- OR ANY OTHER MAN--CAN DO FOR HER. I'M SORRY, JOHN.
YOU'RE WRONG, OLD FRIEND. I CAN DO SOMETHING!
I'VE BEEN WORKING ON MY SERUMS FOR MONTHS NOW. AND THIS ONE, MY SPIDER EXTRACT-- IS THE FULFILLMENT OF ALL THAT WORK.
IF IT WORKS, JESSICA WILL BE ABLE TO SURVIVE THE RADIATION. SHE'LL ADAPT TO IT. SHE'LL LIVE!

COME ON, DARLING-- REACT! YOU'VE GOT TO REACT!
ALL MY WORK, MY HOPES-- THEY'RE ALL CENTERED ON YOU.

IF YOU SURVIVE, MY SERUMS MAY ONE DAY SAVE THE WORLD!

JOHN--?
I-I... OH, LORD, MERIEM... OH MY LORD.
SHE'S NOT RESPONDING.

DIDN'T YOU TELL ME YOUR SERUMS NEEDED A MONTH'S INCUBATION PERIOD?
BLAST IT, JESSICA DOESN'T HAVE A MONTH!
MY DAUGHTER'S DYING, AND IT'S MY FAULT!

NOT NECESSARILY, JOHN. IT'S MY TURN TO HELP NOW-- WITH MY GENETIC ACCELERATOR!
PERHAPS I CAN SPEED UP THE INCUBATION TIME. IT WILL BE RISKY, BUT--
NO! I WON'T HAVE MY DAUGHTER TURNED INTO A GUINEA PIG!
YOU CAN'T HAVE HER! YOU CAN'T!

THEN THERE ARE IMAGES OF JONATHAN DREW COMFORTING HIS FRAGILE WIFE. BUT, IN THE END, THE STRAIN WAS TOO GREAT FOR HER.
...I WILL ALWAYS LOVE YOU, MERIEM. ALWAYS CHERISH YOU.
EVEN AS HER DAUGHTER JESSICA WAS PLACED WITHIN THE GENETIC ACCELERATOR, MERIEM DREW DIED.
MAY YOU REST IN ETERNAL PEACE!

MYSTERIOUSLY, JONATHAN DREW VANISHED. BUT FOR HIS FRIEND, WORK CONTINUED...
INCREDIBLE! THE ACCELERATOR'S BUILDING ON JOHN'S SERUM--IN WAYS I NEVER EXPECTED.

SHE'LL LIVE, BUT I'LL HAVE TO REPEAT THESE TREATMENTS FOR YEARS.
GOD KNOWS WHAT WILL BECOME OF JESSICA DREW BY THEN!

THE YEARS PASSED, AND THE SCIENTIST HIMSELF TOOK ON A NEW IDENTITY. HE WAS NOW-- THE HIGH EVOLUTIONARY... CREATOR OF MIRACLES!*
AND, AT LAST, HIS WORK WITH JESSICA DREW WAS OVER.
SUCCESS. UN-ACCOUNTABLE EONS OF EVOLUTION... ACHIEVED IN MERE MOMENTS!
IN THE PAST I HAVE WROUGHT "NEW MEN" FROM VARIOUS ANIMAL SPECIES. BUT THIS SUCCESS IS UNIQUE COMPARED WITH MY OTHERS.
FOR THIS WAS WAS THE FIRST USE OF A HUMAN BEING IN MY WORK. JESSICA DREW, CHILD OF MY LONG-LOST FRIEND, LIVES... BUT SHE IS NOW HALF SPIDER!
*MARVEL SPOTLIGHT #32 --MARV.

NO! NO! NO! NO
THE VISIONS... THEY'RE OVER, AND ONCE AGAIN THEY SHOW ME FOR WHAT I AM. NEITHER HUMAN NOR SPIDER.
WHILE I WAS WITH THE HIGH EVOLUTIONARY, HIS OTHER CREATURES SHUNNED ME, FOR I WAS A REBORN HUMAN, AND NOT AN ANIMAL. YET, I WAS NOT QUITE HUMAN, EITHER.

I WAS HATED THERE. NO WONDER I FLED WUNDAGORE... TO SEARCH THE WORLD.
BUT, I WAS CAPTURED AGAIN, TRAPPED IN A SECOND PRISON, THIS ONE CONTROLLED BY A GROUP CALLED HYDRA. THEY BRAIN-WASHED ME...
...CONTROLLED ME. I WAS THEIR PUPPET.

BUT I NO LONGER BELONG TO ANYONE. I'M FREE NOW. I'M BY MYSELF AT LAST. BUT, HEAVEN HELP ME, IT STILL MAKES NO DIFFERENCE!
NOW IT'S PEOPLE WHO SHUN ME... PEOPLE WHO RUN FROM ME.

I MAY LOOK AND FEEL HUMAN, BUT I'VE THE BLOOD OF A SPIDER COURSING THROUGH MY VEINS.

I'M A SPIDER-WOMAN, AND WHEREVER I GO, I TAKE THAT DEADLY CURSE WITH ME.

BUT I CAN'T KEEP ON RUNNING. I'M NOT AT HOME WITH THE NEW MEN. I MUST FORCE MYSELF TO BE AT HOME HERE--WITH THE HUMANS.
THIS IS WHERE MY FUTURE LIES!
I'VE SPENT A LIFETIME AWAY FROM PEOPLE. NOW I MUST ADJUST TO THEM, LEARN THEIR WAYS, AND HOPEFULLY BECOME ONE OF THEM!

AND THE FIRST STEP IS TO FIND A JOB--NO MATTER HOW LONG IT TAKES, NO MATTER HOW MANY REJECTIONS I'M GIVEN.
I NEED MONEY TO BUY GROCERIES, TO PAY MY RENT, TO LIVE.
AND STILL MORE, I NEED A JOB TO BE INDEPENDENT, TO LEARN JUST WHO JESSICA DREW IS.
567
Antique

BUT JOBS ARE NOT EASY TO COME BY THESE DAYS, ESPECIALLY FOR A WOMAN WITHOUT A PAST...
I'M SORRY, MISS. I'D LIKE TO HELP YOU, BUT--
--YOU'VE NO BACKGROUND, NO REFERENCES, NO EXPERIENCE!
NO HELP WANTED
ABSOLUTELY NOT, GIRL. THERE IS SOMETHING ABOUT YOU THAT WOULD POSITIVELY FRIGHTEN AWAY MY VALUED CUSTOMERS.
PLEASE LEAVE HERE, IMMEDIATELY!

JESSICA DREW IS BOTH ANGRY AND PUZZLED AS SHE PACES HER WAY DOWN FASHIONABLE OXFORD STREET...
THAT GIRL--? I'D KNOW HER ANYWHERE.
MISS--! STOP--STOP!
HIM? THE MAN FROM THE SUPER-MARKET?
I MUSTN'T LET HIM GET TO ME...NO MATTER WHAT!

I CAN'T LET MY NEW LIFE END, NOT BEFORE IT BEGINS!
PLEASE, DON'T RUN!
I JUST WANT TO TALK TO YOU!

HE'S STILL CHASING ME, STILL HOUNDING ME.
I'M FED UP WITH THIS... ALL OF IT!
I'M REJECTED BY EVERYONE WHO SEES ME. NOW THE POLICE ARE OUT TO CAPTURE ME!

WELL, IF HE WANTS ME, HE'LL HAVE TO PUT UP A GOOD FIGHT!
FROM NOW ON, SPIDER-WOMAN FIGHTS BACK!

THERE YOU ARE. THANK GOODNESS!
I JUST WANTED TO TELL YOU, YOU WERE RIGHT! NOTHING WAS TAKEN FROM THE MARKET.
GET AWAY FROM ME, YOU FOOL.
I WON'T BE HOUNDED! I WON'T BE CAGED EVER AGAIN. NOT BY YOU, NOT BY ANYONE!

THERE IS A BONE-CRUNCHING SNAP, AND A LAMPPOST IS SUDDENLY RIPPED FROM ITS CASING.
NO! WHAT AM I DOING? I'M NOT A MURDERER!
BUT IF THAT POST HITS HIM, I'LL HAVE KILLED HIM!

SHE IS FAST, AND IN THE BLINK OF AN EYE, THIS STRANGELY-COSTUMED FEMALE LEAPS TOWARDS THE SUDDENLY FRIGHTENED JERRY HUNT...
I CAN'T LET YOU DIE, EVEN IF YOU ARE HUNTING ME.
YOU DON'T UNDERSTAND! I--OOOMPHHHH!

PUSHED HIM INTO THE WALL AND KNOCKED HIM OUT.
HE'LL SURVIVE, AND I'LL BE ABLE TO GET AWAY.
BUT, I CAN'T CONTINUE ON LIKE THIS... NOT ANY LONGER.

A WEEK PASSES, THEN TWO MORE. AND FINALLY...
HE KNOWS WHAT I LOOK LIKE BENEATH MY MASK, AND WITH MY REPUTATION AROUND HERE, I WON'T BE TOO DIFFICULT TO TRACK DOWN.
WHICH MEANS I'VE GOT TO DISGUISE MYSELF MORE THAN I ALREADY HAVE.

A LITTLE BLACK HAIR DYE WILL TAKE CARE OF JESSICA DREW, AND I'LL NEED A NEW MASK FOR SPIDER-WOMAN.
THOUGH I'VE STILL GOT TO DECIDE WHY I MUST BE TWO PEOPLE. WHY THERE IS BOTH A JESSICA DREW AND A SPIDER-WOMAN.
HAIR COLOR
I WAS TOLD THERE ARE SUPER-HEROES IN AMERICA WHO KEEP THEIR TRUE IDENTITIES A SECRET... TO PROTECT THEMSELVES, I BELIEVE.
BUT I'M NOT A HERO. I'VE NO INTENTIONS OF BECOMING ONE.

I'M JESSICA DREW, CALLED ARACHNE BY HYDRA, CALLED SPIDER-WOMAN BY ALL OTHERS.
MAYBE... THAT'S WHY I FLIT BACK AND FORTH, WEARING THIS GAUDY COSTUME AND STILL TRY TO PASS FOR NORMAL.
I WAS BORN HUMAN, AND I'VE BECOME SOMETHING DIFFERENT. I AM TWO BEINGS; JESSICA MY HUMAN HALF, SPIDER-WOMAN MY-- EH?

GUNSHOTS? I'D SWEAR THEY'RE COMING FROM PARLIAMENT!

I WAS RIGHT. AND THERE'S THAT COP WHO'S BEEN CHASING ME, PINNED DOWN BY TWO CRIMINALS!
WAIT! I-I REMEMBER THEM! I SAW THEM WHEN WHEN I ATTACKED BEN GRIMM AT WESTMINSTER ABBEY,* AND THEN AGAIN WHEN I MET MODRED.**
*MTIO #29 -- MARV.
**MTIO #33 -- MARV AGAIN!

BACK UP, JERRY. I DON'T LIKE THE LOOK OF THE LASER RIFLES THOSE GUYS ARE SPORTING.
"BACK UP?" YOU'RE JOKING, SID. WE WEREN'T ASSIGNED TO SCOTLAND YARD BY SHIELD TO WORRY ABOUT OUR-SELVES!
WE'VE BEEN AFTER THOSE TWO EVER SINCE THE BOMBINGS BEGAN HERE A FEW WEEKS BACK.*
* MTIO #30 --MARV.

AND I MEAN TO GET THEM, ONE WAY OR AN--
AGGGHHH!
ZWAP
LORD! JERRY'S BEEN HIT!

GET BACK, THESE TWO ARE MINE!
TREVOR LAD-- IT'S THAT DAME AGAIN, THE ONE FROM THE ABBEY!
AND THIS TIME, SHE'S AFTER US!
BLAST! TAKE CARE OF 'ER, CHAUNCY. I GOT ME HANDS FULL WITH THESE BLOODY BOBBIES!

LAD, THE LASER'S NOT STOPPING HER. IT'S NOT STRONG ENOUGH!
MY FATHER'S SERUM! IT WAS DESIGNED TO NULLIFY RADIATION, AND LASER BEAMS ARE STIMULATED RADIATION!
BUT I HAVEN'T TIME TO PLAY WITH THESE TWO. I WANT TO CHECK OUT THAT COP...
THERE'S SOMETHING ABOUT HIM THAT KEEPS DRAWING US TOGETHER.
ZDAK!
MY VENOM BLAST SHOULD PUT THAT ONE AWAY FOR AWHILE.

'EY! WOT YOU DO TO CHAUNCY, LADY?
IF YOU'VE KILLED 'IM...
AT ONE TIME I WOULD HAVE, FOOL. BUT I'VE LEARNED TO TEMPER MY BLASTS.
HE'S MERELY BEEN STUNNED--!

DON'T WORRY, THOUGH. YOU'LL SEE HIM UP SOON ENOUGH.
ONCE YOU AWAKEN FROM SPIDER-WOMAN'S DEADLY STING!
ZDAK

I DON'T KNOW WHY I'M GETTING INVOLVED WITH THIS, BUT WHEN I SAW HIM FALL--
--SOMETHING INSIDE ME WENT HAYWIRE!
I-I DON'T KNOW THIS MAN... YET, FOR SOME REASON, I CARE FOR HIM. WHY? WHY?

THANK HEAVEN, HE'S STILL ALIVE, BUT JUST BARELY. HIS HEART'S SLOWING DOWN WITH EVERY BEAT.
HE'S DYING... IN MY ARMS, HE'S DYING!
HE'S A STRANGER TO ME, YET, I DON'T WANT HIM TO DIE. I DON'T WANT TO SEE HIM HURT IN--
--SOMEONE BEHIND ME! MY VENOM BLAST MUST HAVE WORN OFF SOONER THAN I EXPECTED.
WHICH MEANS NEXT TIME I CAN FIRE A MORE CONCENTRATED BLAST.

HAVE TO BE CAREFUL. SOMETHING TELLS ME HE'S AIMING HIS GUN... HAVE TO SPIN...
NOW!
OH NO! I ALMOST UNLEASHED TOO MUCH ENERGY. ANY MORE AND I WOULD HAVE KILLED HIM.
I SAID I HAD NO TIME FOR GAMES, FOOL. DID YOU THINK I WAS JOKING?
IT'S MY TEMPER... I ALMOST LET IT GET OUT OF HAND. I ALMOST BECAME A MURDERER!

AM I CURSED NEVER TO FORGET THAT I'M TWO BEINGS?
TWO BEINGS FOREVER AT WAR WITH MYSELF!
HEAVEN HELP ME, I'M BOTH HUMAN AND SPIDER, AND AS SUCH-- LESS THAN EITHER!
WITH ONE HAND I EMBRACE LIFE. WITH THE OTHER I WIELD DEATH!
BUT, I CAN NOT ALLOW ANYONE TO STOP ME, NOT UNTIL I'M SURE THIS MAN LIVES!
STAND BACK, ALL OF YOU. YOU'VE SEEN MY POWER. DON'T FORCE ME TO UNLEASH IT!
STAND ASIDE WHILE I TAKE THIS ONE WITH ME!

YOU CRAZY, LADY? WE CAN'T PERMIT SUCH AN--
NO! DON'T STOP HER... DON'T ST--
HE'S TRYING TO SPEAK... TO WARN THEM AWAY.
I CAN HEAR THE WEAKNESS IN HIS VOICE. IF I DON'T HELP HIM SOON, HE'LL DIE!

AND I KNOW HIS DEATH WILL BE ON MY HANDS!
I SAID-- GET AWAY FROM ME!
WHAK

IF YOU WANT HIM TO LIVE, GIVE HIM TO ME!
I'M HIS ONLY CHANCE... HIS ONLY HOPE OF REACHING HELP IN TIME.

EPILOGUE:
LONDON HOSPITAL...
I-I STILL DON'T UNDER-STAND...
THAT STRANGE WOMAN SAVED YOUR LIFE, JERRY. SHE FORCED THE DOCTORS TO USE HER BLOOD. SHE INSISTED IT WOULD HELP YOU RESIST THE LASER RADIATION.

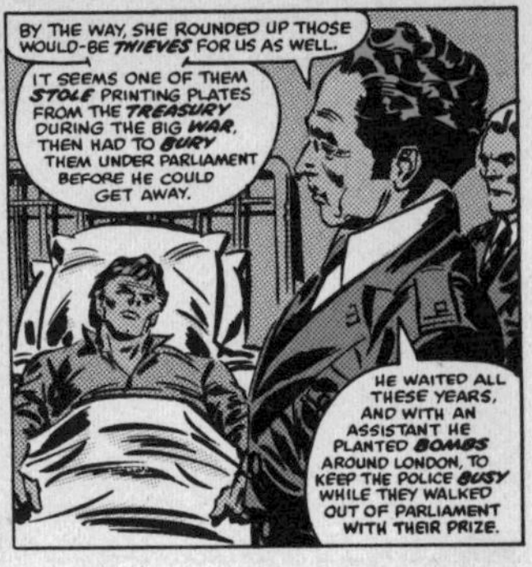
BY THE WAY, SHE ROUNDED UP THOSE WOULD-BE THIEVES FOR US AS WELL.
IT SEEMS ONE OF THEM STOLE PRINTING PLATES FROM THE TREASURY DURING THE BIG WAR, THEN HAD TO BURY THEM UNDER PARLIAMENT BEFORE HE COULD GET AWAY.
HE WAITED ALL THESE YEARS, AND WITH AN ASSISTANT HE PLANTED BOMBS AROUND LONDON, TO KEEP THE POLICE BUSY WHILE THEY WALKED OUT OF PARLIAMENT WITH THEIR PRIZE.

UNFORTUNATELY FOR THEM, THEY FORGOT ONE SMALL DETAIL, YOU SEE, THOUGH THE PLATES COULD PRINT UNTOLD BILLIONS OF BRITISH POUNDS--
--THEY WERE PLATES FOR THE OLD POUND. BRITAIN CONVERTED TO A NEW POUND SEVERAL YEARS BACK. IN OTHER WORDS, JERRY-- THEY SHOULD HAVE STAYED IN BED!
BY THE WAY, I TOLD YOUR SUPERIORS AT SHIELD ALL ABOUT IT, AND YOU'LL NEVER GUESS WHAT FURY SAID. JERRY? JERRY?
SHE SAVED ME? SHE FOUGHT THOSE THIEVES FOR ME, THEN SHE GAVE ME HER BLOOD?
MORE THAN THAT, I'M STILL SURE I KNOW HER FROM SOME-WHERE, BUT I CAN'T REMEMBER WHERE.

CLARENCE, DON'T ASK ME TO EX-PLAIN IT, I CAN'T. CERTAINLY NOT RATION-ALLY, BUT WITHOUT KNOWING ANYTHING ABOUT THAT WOMAN, I WANT HER.
AND YOU KNOW WHAT'S WORSE? I DON'T KNOW IF IT'S TO STOP HER OR TO LOVE HER.
BUT, I WANT THAT WOMAN MORE THAN I'VE WANTED ANY WOMAN IN MY LIFE.
WHOEVER SHE IS, I WANT SPIDER-WOMAN!
NEXT:
WHAT IS IN STORE FOR JESSICA DREW? IS THERE A FUTURE FOR A WOMAN WITHOUT A PAST? SEE FOR YOURSELF, AS SPIDER-WOMAN MUST BATTLE: EXCALIBER and MORGAN LE FEY! DON'T MISS IT!

Stan Lee PRESENTS: THE MYSTERIOUS SPIDER-WOMAN!

MARY WOLFMAN WRITER/EDITOR • CARMINE INFANTINO PENCILS • TONY DE ZUNIGA INKS • IRV WATANABE LETTERS • JANICE COHEN COLORS

SO STRANGE, I'M SEARCHING FOR CLUES TO MY FATHER'S IDENTITY...
...WHEN I'VE YET TO LEARN MY OWN!
BUT I'VE TRACED HIM TO THIS MUSEUM ...HE WORKED HERE AFTER MY MOTHER DIED. BUT EVEN IF I FIND HIM--HOW WILL THAT MAKE ME ANY DIFFERENT?
I SHOULD LEARN WHO I AM... WHY I AM!
I SHOULD LEARN WHETHER I'M THE WOMAN HE NAMED JESSICA DREW ...OR THE NIGHT-PROWLING CREATURE WHO'S BEEN CALLED SPIDER-WOMAN!

C'MON, GET ON WITH IT... MOVE ON, LADY.
I JUST WANT TA ROB THIS HERE SPOOK HOUSE AN' GET OUT!
THAT AIN'T TOO MUCH FER AN UP-AN'-COMIN' THIEF TA ASK FOR, IS IT?
SHOVE OFF, AN' LET ME GET ABOUT MY BUSINESS!

"MORGAN LE FAY'S EXCALIBUR--" THE ONE THAT ARTHUR'S SISTER FORGED AND USED TO REPLACE HIS OWN SWORD.
WHEN HE USED IT IN BATTLE, HE LOST... AT LEAST IF I REMEMBER THE LEGENDS CORR--
MORGAN LE FAY'S EXCALIBUR

WAIT! I'VE NEVER READ MALLORY'S ARTHURIAN STORIES... I'VE NEVER READ ANY SOURCE BOOKS. YET, I INSTINCTIVELY KNOW...
ALL RIGHT, LITTLE LADY--I SUGGEST YOU PUT UP YOUR HANDS ...YOU'RE CAUGHT!
TOO BUSY WORRYING ABOUT MYSELF. I DIDN'T HEAR...

DON'T BUDGE, LADY... NOT EVEN TO POWDER YOUR PRETTY FACE.
WE'VE CAUGHT YOU RED-HANDED!
S-SIR...LOOK AT HER...SHE'S GRINNIN' LIKE A DEVIL, SIR...

SHE AIN'T MOVIN'-- BUT SOMEHOW SHE'S SPOOKIN' ME...MAKIN' MY KNEES KNOCK TOGETHER LIKE CHEAP DRUMS, SIR.
L-LOOK AT HER EYES ...THEY'RE DRAWIN' ME TO HER... SIR!
I-- I KNOW WHAT YOU MEAN... C-CAN'T MOVE...

BLAST--! SOMEHOW THAT WITCH IS HYPNOTIZ-ING US!
SLAPPER, YA GOT YERSELF INTA QUITE A FIX THIS TIME ...NOW THE COPS'RE HERE. AIN'T NO WAY YER EVER GONNA GET OUTTA THIS IN ONE PIECE.
JUST YER LUCK--YA WANTED TA BREAK INTA A MUSEUM--AN' YA FOUND YERSELF A NUT-HOUSE, INSTEAD!

S-SIR... SHE'S GETTIN' AWAY--FLYIN' OUTTA THE ROOM!
PLEASE, SIR, TELL ME THIS AIN'T HAPPENIN'-- TELL ME THAT BIRDS LIKE HER CAN'T FLY!
TELL ME ANYTHIN', SIR--I THINK I'M GOIN' CRACKERS!

I WISH I COULD, GEOFFREY...BUT SHE'S REAL...AND IT'S UP TO US TO FIND HER.
BUT AFTER WE'RE DONE HERE...REMIND ME TO TURN IN MY BADGE AND TAKE UP ALUMINUM SIDING!

THANK YA, LORD. AS SURE AS I'M BROKE AN' STARVIN', I THOUGHT I WAS DONE FOR!
BUT, YA GIVEN ME A SECOND CHANCE, AN' I'LL BE TAKIN' IT...
...ALONG WITH THAT SWORD THE LITTLE LADY WAS LOOKIN' OVER.
"SLAPPER" STRUTHERS IS NOT A NICE MAN. AT THE AGE OF SIX, HE ROLLED HIS FIRST DRUNK.
AT 12, HE ROBBED HIS FIRST GROCERY STORE. AT 18, HE KNIFED HIS FIRST VICTIM.

THEREFORE, DO NOT PITY HIM FOR THE PAIN HE SUDDENLY FEELS SHOOTING THROUGH HIS BODY AS HE GRASPS THE ANCIENT SWORD. HE HAS EARNED THE DEVASTATING TORTURE...
AT LAST...I HAVE A MAN TOTALLY WITHOUT COMPASSION...A MAN WHO CAN BE CONTROLLED...
BUT, AS THE ELECTRICAL FORCE WORMS ITS WAY THROUGH HIM, HE HEARS A VOICE... A SOFT, MOANING ECHO FILTERING THROUGH THE CENTURIES...
...BY THE PSYCHIC AND SORCEROUS POWERS OF-- MORGAN LE FAY!
KNOW THIS, HUMAN-OF-ANOTHER-TIME... I AM THE SISTER OF ARTHUR PENDRAGON, GREATEST WARRIOR-KING OF ALL. I CONJURED THIS SWORD FROM THE PITS OF HELL ITSELF--

--AND PRAYED WHEN ARTHUR WIELDED IT-- THAT HE WOULD DIE.

BUT ARTHUR SURVIVED ...AND MY SWORD LAY BROKEN IN RUIN...UNTIL I RE-FORGED THE WEAPON AND INSTILLED WITHIN IT THE POWERS OF THE BLACK ARTS...

...WHICH I NOW HAND DOWN TO YOU!

"SLAPPER" CANNOT MOVE WHILE THE VOICE SPEAKS. BUT, THEN...
YOU HEAR THAT SCREAM? COULD THE WOMAN HAVE DOUBLED BACK, AND...?
LORD!
MY GOD--GEOFFREY!

S-SIR...I SEE IT PLAIN AS DAY, BUT--PLEASE...TELL ME IT ISN'T HAPPENING...
...TELL ME I'M A BLINKING LOONIE RAVING HALF OUT OF MY MIND!
PLEASE, SIR--TELL ME ANY-THING...I'LL BELIEVE IT...I

...ANYTHING IS BETTER THAN BELIEVING A MAN COULD TURN INTO...THAT!
GREAT QUEEN, THY BLACK ARTS ARE AS OMNIPOTENT AS EVER.

THY SERVANT NOW OCCUPIES THE BODY OF THE HUMAN WRETCH...
...AND WIELDS THY POWER AS IF THOU HADST BRIDGED THE CENTURIES, THYSELF!
SZAAKKK
SIR! HIS SWORD...
ARRGHH!

SCREAMS? THE POLICEMEN ARE IN TROUBLE!
BUT THAT DOES NOT INVOLVE ME.
I'VE NO REASON TO AID MY PURSUERS. I MUST BE CONCERNED WITH ME! ONLY ME!

BUT-- I CAN'T BE. IF I'M TO END THE CURSE OF BEING MORE SPIDER THAN WOMAN...
...I'VE NO CHOICE BUT TO GET INVOLVED!
INTRUDER, EH? AND A FEMALE ONE AT THAT!

WHAT, QUEEN? DESTROY HER, YOU SAY? SHE WIELDS AN INCREDIBLE POWER?
ZZZZAKKK
WHAT DOES THAT MATTER--WHEN EXCALIBER HAS POWERS OF HIS OWN?!

HE CALLS HIMSELF EXCALIBER --TALKS TO SOME UNSEEN FORCE.
WHAT HAVE I GOTTEN INVOLVED WITH? WHO AM I FACING?

YOU'VE BEEN GRANTED YOUR POWERS FOR A REASON-- DO NOT HESITATE WITH THIS ONE.
FINISH HER... AND BE OFF!
HE FIRES TOO WIDE...HIS BLAST WILL STRIKE THAT POLICEMAN!
IF THAT IS YOUR WISH, QUEEN-- SO BE IT!

HUNH? WHAT'S GOING--?
ARRRGGHH!
SHE IS DOWN...NOW, GO--

I HEAR ... AND OBEY!

HE'S FLEEING ...BUT...I HAVEN'T THE STRENGTH TO FOLLOW...
I...I JUST WANT TO GO HOME...HOME...

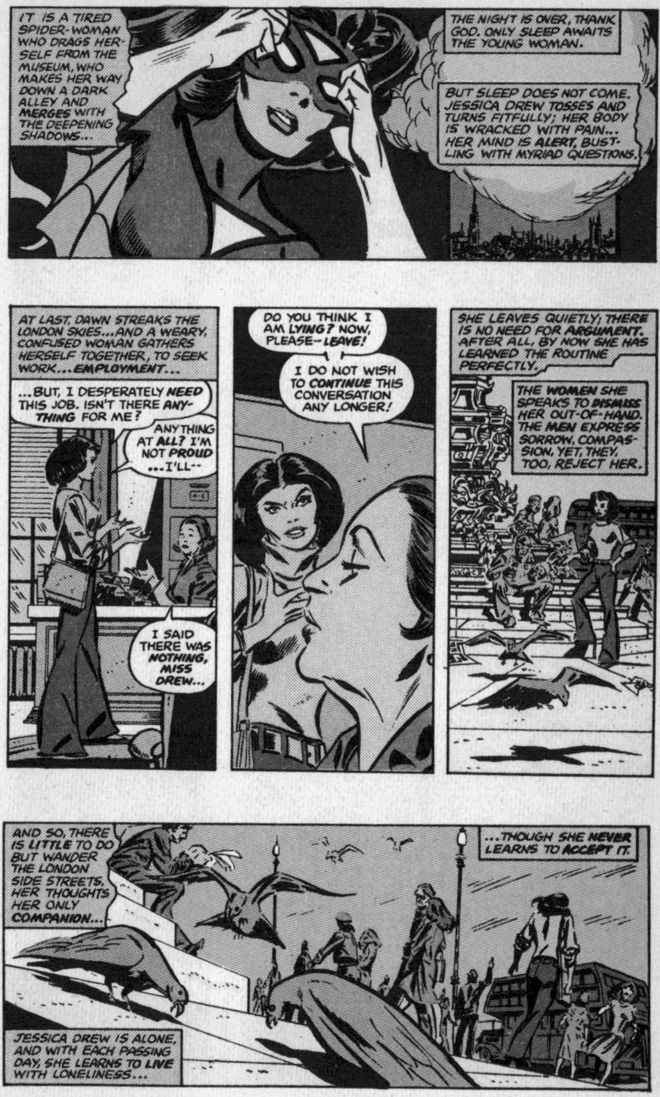

AT LAST, DAWN STREAKS THE LONDON SKIES...AND A WEARY, CONFUSED WOMAN GATHERS HERSELF TOGETHER, TO SEEK WORK...EMPLOYMENT...

...BUT, I DESPERATELY NEED THIS JOB. ISN'T THERE ANYTHING FOR ME?

ANYTHING AT ALL? I'M NOT PROUD ...I'LL--

I SAID THERE WAS NOTHING, MISS DREW...

DO YOU THINK I AM LYING? NOW, PLEASE--LEAVE!

I DO NOT WISH TO CONTINUE THIS CONVERSATION ANY LONGER!

SHE LEAVES QUIETLY; THERE IS NO NEED FOR ARGUMENT. AFTER ALL, BY NOW SHE HAS LEARNED THE ROUTINE PERFECTLY.

THE WOMEN SHE SPEAKS TO DISMISS HER OUT-OF-HAND. THE MEN EXPRESS SORROW, COMPASSION. YET, THEY, TOO, REJECT HER.

I...I KNOW WHAT MY PROBLEM IS-- I SPENT MY WHOLE LIFE WITH THE HIGH EVOLUTIONARY... LOOKED AWAY IN SOME PLASTIC CHAMBER UNTIL HE FOUND A WAY TO CURE THE RADIATION POISONING THAT WAS KILLING ME--!
CLOTHE
BAIT
GIRLS ONLY

I...I NEVER SPOKE WITH PEOPLE... IS IT ANY WONDER THEY SENSE HOW UNCOMFORTABLE I BECOME WHEN I AM WITH THEM NOW?
TERRY TOPS
TATTLE TALE JEANS
JANINE OLE JEANS
TOPS
MY GOD-- I'M A FULL-GROWN WOMAN, YET I KNOW AS LITTLE ABOUT LIFE AS IF I'D JUST STEPPED FROM THE WOMB!

AND...PEOPLE KNOW THAT... THEY SENSE IT...AND, HEAVEN HELP ME--THEY AVOID ME BECAUSE OF IT.

WHAT MAKES IT WORSE-- THERE IS NO WAY I CAN EVER CHANGE HOW THEY FEEL ABOUT ME... NO WAY I CAN--
MAGNUS SPECIALIST IN THE SUPER NATURAL
A READING, LASS? LEARNING THE FUTURE WILL SOOTHE AWAY YOUR PRESENT TROUBLES.
PLEASE ENTER MY SHOP, THERE ARE MANY CURIOS WITHIN THAT WILL FASCINATE YOU.
CARDS
PALM READ
MAGIC

FOR HERE, IN MAGNUS' SHOP, ALL SHADOWS DIFFUSE WITH LIGHT ...ALL PAINS WASH AWAY WITH LOVE.

PLEASE, MY DEAR MISS DREW-- ENTER. I PROMISE YOU WILL NOT REGRET YOUR DECISION.
YOU KNOW MY NAME? BUT-- HOW?

KNOWLEDGE FLOWS ON THE CURRENTS OF TIME, AND ALL CURRENTS FLOW THROUGH ME.
I LOOK AT YOU AND KNOW YOU ARE A STRANGER...NOT ONLY TO THIS CITY--
--BUT TO...THE WORLD!
YOU ARE SEARCHING FOR IDENTITY... YOUR OWN...AND, I SEE...A RELATIVE'S... A CLOSE ONE. YOUR FATHER!
YOU SEE ALL THIS BY READING MY PALM?
TOLKIEN

BY READING YOUR EYES, MY DEAR--FOR THEY MIRROR YOUR SOUL AND REVEAL ALL TO ONE WHO UNDERSTANDS THEIR MEANING.
WHAT ELSE DO YOU SEE?

A FRIGHTENED GIRL WITHIN A WOMAN'S BODY. A GIRL STUMBLING IN THE DARKNESS, GROPING FOR AN ANSWER.
BUT IT IS AN ANSWER YOU'LL NOT FIND HERE.
WHERE? WHERE IS THE ANSWER? TELL ME--!

SCOTLAND YARD...
DAMN! IT'S BEEN TWO WEEKS, AND I HAVEN'T A SINGLE CLUE.
I THOUGHT SCOTLAND YARD COULD BE EXPECTED TO FIND A SINGLE WOMAN IN LONDON. WHAT IN BLAZES IS TAKING SO LONG?
BAM!
YOU'VE BEEN EDGY ALL WEEK, JERRY. CALM DOWN... NOTHING IS WORTH THE AGGRAVATION YOU'RE GOING THROUGH.
FRANK, OLD BUDDY, I'LL BE PLEASED AS HELL TO TAKE IT EASY--AFTER WE'VE FOUND THIS WOMAN--
--AFTER I'VE HAD THE CHANCE TO SPEAK TO THIS... SPIDER-WOMAN!
I--I WANT HER!

FOR WHAT, JERRY? YOU DON'T KNOW WHO SHE IS...OR WHY SHE WEARS THAT BIZARRE COSTUME.
WHAT DOES SHE MEAN TO YOU?

I THINK I LOVE HER, FRANK.
THAT'S WHAT SHE MEANS TO ME.

THE UNDERGROUND...
SOMETHIN'S AILIN' YOU, SLAPPER...? SOMETHIN' REAL BAD! YER HAVIN' STRANGE NIGHTMARES...
MAYBE YOU SHOULD SEE A DOC ...HAVE 'IM OPEN UP YER HEAD AN' SEE WHAT'S MAKIN' IT GO CRACKERS?
'CAUSE, WHAT I THOUGHT HAPPENED TO ME...IS JUST PLAIN IMPOSSIBLE. IT--

HUNN? SOMETHIN'S PUSHING ME...

"SLAPPER" STRUTHERS FALLS TO THE TRACKS... BUT HE DOES NOT RISE. INSTEAD, A GREEN CLAD FIGURE STANDS ERECT--
--A MAN DEFINITELY OUT OF TIME.
I HAVE RETURNED, MORGAN LE FAY... THY POWER HAST SET ME FREE ONCE MORE!

AYE, MILADY, 'TIS MOST CERTAIN THAT I BOW TO THEE AND WORSHIP THY POWER AND THY BEAUTY!
THY MOST NOBLE KNIGHT AND SERVANT COMMENDS HIS SPIRIT TO THEE--
--AND MORE, HE SHALL FIGHT FOR THEE, E'EN SHOULD HE DIE MOST IGNOBLY!

A DRAGON, MY QUEEN? A TEST TO PROVE MY LOYALTY! MILADY, I ACCEPT--
--AND SHALL VANQUISH MY FOE WITH THE LUST OF BATTLE IGNITING MY SOUL!

THE STEEL DRAGON ROARS WITH ELECTRICAL FEROCITY. BUT THE FLAMING SWORD EXCALIBUR ATTACKS THE CHARGING BEAST WITH A FURY ALL ITS OWN!
SKRAKKK
WHILE, FROM MANY HUNDREDS OF YEARS PAST...

HALT, EXCALIBER... CEASE YOUR FRUITLESS RAGING!
YOU ARE MY KNIGHT... BUT YOU MUST UNDERSTAND THE WORLD YOU NOW WALK.
PERMIT THE MIND OF THE HUMAN YOU INHABIT TO CO-EXIST WITH YOUR OWN!
I HEAR YOUR WORDS, MY QUEEN... THE EXCALIBER NOW WALKS AS TWO MEN!
HASTILY, HE LEAVES THE UNDERGROUND AND SEES A PROUD STEED RIPE FOR HIS OWN USE.
THE POLICE OFFICER RIDING THE HORSE FINDS HIMSELF SUDDENLY DISMOUNTED.

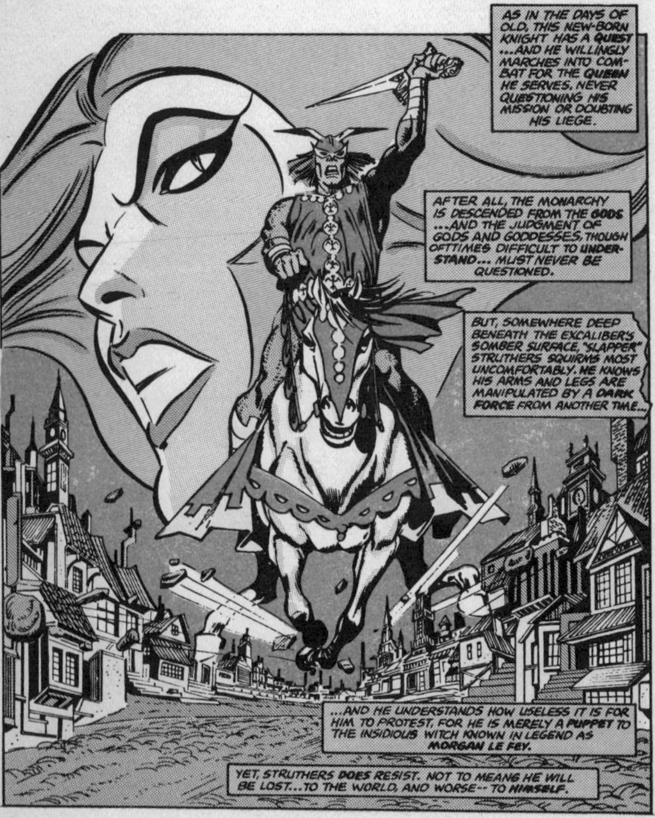

AS IN THE DAYS OF OLD, THIS NEW-BORN KNIGHT HAS A QUEST ...AND HE WILLINGLY MARCHES INTO COMBAT FOR THE QUEEN HE SERVES, NEVER QUESTIONING HIS MISSION OR DOUBTING HIS LIEGE.

AFTER ALL, THE MONARCHY IS DESCENDED FROM THE GODS ...AND THE JUDGMENT OF GODS AND GODDESSES, THOUGH OFTTIMES DIFFICULT TO UNDERSTAND... MUST NEVER BE QUESTIONED.

BUT, SOMEWHERE DEEP BENEATH THE EXCALIBER'S SOMBER SURFACE, "SLAPPER" STRUTHERS SQUIRMS MOST UNCOMFORTABLY. HE KNOWS HIS ARMS AND LEGS ARE MANIPULATED BY A DARK FORCE FROM ANOTHER TIME...

...AND HE UNDERSTANDS HOW USELESS IT IS FOR HIM TO PROTEST, FOR HE IS MERELY A PUPPET TO THE INSIDIOUS WITCH KNOWN IN LEGEND AS MORGAN LE FEY.

YET, STRUTHERS DOES RESIST. NOT TO MEANS HE WILL BE LOST...TO THE WORLD, AND WORSE-- TO HIMSELF.

THE DARKLY LIT APARTMENT OF JESSICA DREW...
...HE SAID MY DESTINY LIES IN AMERICA... THAT MY SEARCH SHOULD BEGIN THERE.
SUCH A STRANGE OLD MAN. HE SAID SO VERY LITTLE, YET... I--I FEEL THAT I'VE LEARNED SO VERY MUCH.
MEEROOOW

A KITTEN? HOW DID YOU FIND YOUR WAY UP HERE, LITTLE ONE?
NO ANSWER? ARE YOU A-AFRAID OF ME? N-NO...YOU'RE JUST A SHY LITTLE THING, AREN'T YOU? SHY, AND A BIT BEWILDERED.
IT'S SUCH A NOISY WORLD, ISN'T IT, LITTLE ONE? NOISY, A BIT FRIGHTENING...AND VERY, VERY LONELY.

BUT, YOU'RE WELCOME TO STAY WITH ME. WE MAY AS WELL BE LONELY--TOGETHER.
AMERICA--? PERHAPS. BUT I WANT--NEED--TO ASK THAT OLD MAN SOMETHING MORE.

SHE WALKS THROUGH LONDON VERY MUCH UNCERTAIN. BUT, SHE IS DETERMINED TO HAVE ANSWERS... AT LEAST TO SOME OF HER MANY PLAGUING QUESTIONS. BUT...
THE STREET IS EMPTY OF ITS TOURISTS. YET, POSED BEFORE THE STRANGE OCCULT SHOP CRAMMED BETWEEN THE ENDLESS ROWS OF CLOTHING STORES...
EXCALIBER? HERE--? IS THERE SOME CONNECTION BETWEEN MAGNUS AND HIM?

JESSICA DREW STEPS INTO THE SHADOWS. SHE WOULD BE USELESS IN COMBAT WITH THE EXCALIBER, BUT WHAT EMERGES FROM THE DEEP BLACKNESS IS A DARK-SHROUDED VIXEN--
--THE SPIDER-WOMAN!
SHE IS ALWAYS READY FOR BATTLE.

WHY ARE YOU HERE?
HER VOICE IS STRONG, DETERMINED, EVEN FRIGHTENING TO HEAR.
THE MAIDEN STRIKES AGAIN?
I THOUGHT YOU HAD LEARNED YOUR LESSON!

BUT, IF YOU HAVE NOT--
WHAM

--THEN, LET THE EXCALIBER SING ITS DEATH-SONG ONCE MORE!
FWOOSH

MY VENOM-BLAST DOESN'T STOP HIM? BUT--HOW? WHY?

NOW, MAGNUS --WHERE HAVE YOU HIDDEN MY MISTRESS' BOOK? SHE MUST HOLD IT ONCE AGAIN!
WHY? SO SHE CAN SPAN THE CENTURIES AND LAY THIS MODERN WORLD TO RUIN?
I REFUSE YOUR QUEEN'S REQUEST.
HER DEMONIC USE OF THE BLACK ARTS MUST NEVER AGAIN BE ALLOWED!

SPIDER-WOMAN IS PUZZLED BY THE TWO MEN. DO THEY KNOW EACH OTHER? MAGNUS SPEAKS AS IF HE DOES, YET...
THERE ARE SO MANY THINGS SPIDER-WOMAN DOES NOT KNOW, AND THE THOUGHT OF THAT FRIGHTENS HER.

SCOTLAND YARD...
JERRY, THINK YOU'D BETTER HEAR THIS. SOME SORT OF FRACAS DOWN ON CARNABY STREET... SOMETHING ABOUT A BLOKE ON A HORSE.
...AND A STRANGELY-GARBED WOMAN!
I THINK SHE MAY BE YOUR BIRD!
MAX, IF SHE IS, I OWE YOU. THANKS!

SHE RISES FROM THE FLAMES, FILING HER QUESTIONS AWAY FOR ANOTHER--A MORE CONVENIENT--TIME.
FOR NOW, THE EXCALIBER MUST BE STOPPED. THAT IS HER FIRST PRIORITY.

YOU MUST BE INSANE, WOMAN! WHY ATTACK ONE WHO ONLY HUMILIATES YOU?

BUT, IF THAT IS YOUR DESIRE-- SO BE IT!
COME, PIT YOUR OWN PRECIOUS POWERS--AGAINST MY MYSTICAL MIGHT...

...AND WE SHALL SEE WHO EMERGES VICTORIOUS...
...AND WHO LIES HUMBLED BY IT ALL!
KRASH

YOUR WARRIOR FALLS, MAGNUS. YOU ARE ALONE.
AND NOW... THE BOOK. WHERE IS IT?
I CANNOT GIVE IT TO HER. AND MORGAN LE FEY KNOWS THAT.
SHE HAS TRIED TO TAKE IT FROM ME COUNTLESS TIMES BEFORE.
BUT, SHE WILL NEVER POSSESS IT, NOT AS LONG AS I LIVE!

WHICH WILL NOT BE MUCH LONGER, OLD MAN.
KEEP TALKING MAGNUS -- DISTRACT HIM...
...UNTIL MY SPEAR KNOCKS THAT DAMNABLE SWORD FROM HIS HAND.

KRAK
WHAT? MY QUEEN! HELP ME! ...HELP ME!

DON'T TRY IT, EXCALIBER. YOU'LL NOT REACH YOUR SWORD ...ALIVE.
YOUR STAND IN MY WAY? MOVE, WOMAN... I MUST GRASP ITS HILT AGAIN!
YOU DON'T KNOW... YOU CAN'T UNDER-STAND WHAT WILL HAPPEN IF I FAIL TO...

NO! IT IS ALREADY TOO LATE!
MY QUEEN...USE YOUR BLACK ARTS PRESERVE YOUR KNIGHT!
M--MILADY...MILADY! DOST THOU ABANDON THINE EVER-LOYAL SERVANT E'ER HE MAY--
LORD! I--HAVE TO... FREE MYSELF...HELP ME, LORD--HELP ME BECOME MYSELF...
...CAN'T... CAN'T BE TWO MEN ANYMORE... CAN'T BE--

YOU WILL NO LONGER BE THAT WAY...
...EVER AGAIN!
THOK

MAGNUS, YOU MUST EXPLAIN. I CANNOT UNDERSTAND...
THERE IS NOTHING TO UNDERSTAND, YOUNG ONE. MORGAN LE FAY AND I ARE...OLD ENEMIES, THAT IS ALL.
BUT, SHE LIVED CENTURIES AGO. SHE-
SO--?
MY DEAR, LET US GO. WE'RE NO LONGER NEEDED HERE.

JEANS
OL' TOPS
BUT, WHAT OF YOUR SHOP? WHAT OF--IT'S GONE? THERE'S JUST A CLOTHING STORE--
EVERYTHING I AM...I TAKE WITH ME.

NOW, AMERICA AWAITS US.
US? YOU'RE COMING WITH ME?
FOR THE PRESENT, OUR DESTINIES FLOW ALONG THE SAME CURRENT.
WE MUST TRAVEL THEM TOGETHER.
NOW COME...THERE IS LITTLE TIME TO PREPARE YOU...FOR THE FUTURE.

HE IGNORES THE EVENING CHILL THOUGH IT NIPS AT HIM THROUGH HIS LIGHT SPRING JACKET--FOR JERRY HUNT'S MIND IS SET ONLY ON SPIDER-WOMAN!
NOTHING? THIS IS THE CORRECT ADDRESS, ISN'T IT?
1417

YES SIR, BUT ALL I SEE IS A CLOTHING STORE. NO HORSE AND CERTAINLY NO WOMAN.
BUT, SHE WAS HERE. I...SENSE THAT! SHE WAS HERE... AND SHE'S GONE.

AND SOMETHING TELLS ME, SHE WILL NOT BE BACK HERE. SOMETHING-- EH?
AMERICA
SPIDER-WOMAN

FRANK, WILL YOU DO ME A COUPLE OF FAVORS?
SIR?

TAKE THIS GUY DOWN TO THE YARD...I'M CERTAIN HE'S GUILTY OF SOMETHING. AND...ONE MORE THING.
YES, SIR?
BOOK ME ON THE FIRST FLIGHT TO AMERICA...AND TELL SHIELD I'M TAKING AN EXTENDED LEAVE OF ABSENCE!
NEXT: A MACABRE NEW VILLAIN! BROTHER GRIMM!

Stan Lee PRESENTS: THE MYSTERIOUS SPIDER-WOMAN!

MARV WOLFMAN WRITER/EDITOR · CARMINE INFANTINO PENCILS · TONY DEZUNIGA INKS · JOE GENOVESE LETTERS · MICHELE WOLFMAN COLORS

THE PERIL OF... BROTHER GRIMM

NOBODY ASKED HOW HE GOT INSIDE. NOBODY DARED ASK. BUT SILENTLY HE MADE HIS WAY TO THE HIGH CATWALK AND WAITED FOR THE PLAY TO BEGIN.

THE MUSIC SOFTENS, ALLOWING THE WITCH TO MUTTER AWAY IN A LOUD STAGE WHISPER. BUT SWELLING UP FROM BEHIND THE PLAYERS IS A GRATING DISHARMONY... A LOUD, RAUCOUS, EAR-SPLITTING WHINE...
...WHICH, LIKE CHALK SCRATCHING ON A BLACKBOARD, IS SHATTERING TO THE SENSES.
THEN, SUDDENLY, ALL IS SILENT...

...AS THE MUSIC IS REPLACED WITH A CLOUD OF AMBER SMOKE.
POOF
AH HA! GOOD DAY, YOU PETTY LITTLE CRETINS!
SKAK
HEY! DON'T LOOK SO SHOCKED, MY PRETTIES. I'VE ONLY COME TO FINISH WHAT YOUR WICKED WITCH BEGAN!

YOU SEE, MY UGLIES--SHE WOULD HAVE MERELY ROASTED YOU TO A WELL-DONE CRISP... AND YOU LOOK SO MUCH MORE DELECTABLE DEHYDRATED!
TRA-LA! ALL SERVED TO PERFECTION BY-- BROTHER GRIMM!

BUT THEN...
YOU THERE, DON'T MOVE--NOT EVEN AN INCH!
IF YOU'VE KILLED THOSE ACTORS, I'LL--
TSK, TSK-- A GENDARME-- A MOUNTIE--SOMEONE OF THE COPPISH PERSUASION! DIDN'T YOUR DEAR OLD MOTHER TEACH YOU MANNERS, MY BLUE-SUITED FRIEND?
IT IS VERY IMPOLITE TO POINT--ESPECIALLY WITH A PISTOL!
AFTER ALL, YOU NEVER KNOW WHO'S GOING TO POINT SOMETHING BACK AT YOU!

SKAK
OR NEED I REALLY POINT THAT OUT, EH? HA HAH!

OH, MY GOD!
OH SHUSH, BUTTER-BALL! YOUR GOD IS PROBABLY PORKY PIG!
NOW THEN, MY GOD IS MONEY--YOU KNOW, SHEKELS, CASH--THE BIG GREEN CHEESE!

SPEAKING OF WHICH, DO HAND OVER ALL OF YOURS! OR WOULD YOU LIKE TO GO BYE-BYE, TOO?
OH, YES, DON'T FORGET THE BOX OFFICE RECEIPTS TO THIS CHARITY CHARADE. AHHH, I SEE YOU HAVEN'T FORGOTTEN. GOOD--GOOD!

PLEASE--TAKE IT ALL--THE MONEY, THE JEWELS, EVERYTHING! JUST DON'T DO TO US WHATEVER YOU DID TO--THE OTHERS.
PERISH THE THOUGHT, MONSIEUR. I NEVER BITE THE HAND THAT FEEDS M-- OOPS! KEEP YOUR PALTRY LOOT, MISTER MANAGER--BROTHER GRIMM SUDDENLY HAS A BETTER, MORE PROFITABLE IDEA!
AH, YA, AH DO, PARDNUH--SU TAKE BACK YER BAUBLES, AND I'LL BE OFF!

TOODLE-OO, TOOTS--I'LL BE SEEIN' YOOTS!
POOF
HE'S GONE--AND HE DIDN'T TAKE A THING!
SOMEONE, ANYONE--PLEASE TELL ME WHAT JUST HAPPENED!

THE BEDROOM OF CONGRESSMAN JAMES T. WYATT
WYATT!

SOMEONE BREAKING IN--? WELL, HE'LL FIND OUT I'M PREPARED FOR--
KRASHH

PUT THAT TOY DOWN, YOU FOOL! I'M NOT HERE TO PLAY GAMES!
KIKK
WH-WHO ARE YOU? WHY ARE YOU--?
I'LL DO THE TALKING, CONGRESSMAN. YOU REMEMBER THE PRIVATE "BUSINESS TRIP" YOU MADE LAST WEEK--THE ONE WITH TAXPAYERS' MONEY?

IT WASN'T SO PRIVATE, CONGRESSMAN. AND I'VE OTHER, MORE INTERESTING PHOTOS THAT CAN PROVE THAT.
ALL RIGHT, WHAT DO YOU WANT FROM ME?
A BUSINESSMAN--GOOD. IT MAKES THIS DIRTY GAME EASIER. I DEMAND $50,000 IN CASH--NOW!

YOU'RE INSANE! I DON'T KEEP THAT KIND OF CASH ON HAND. IT'S IN THE BANK.
THEN I SUGGEST WE MAKE A WITHDRAWAL RIGHT NOW, CONGRESSMAN.
SHORTLY...

I-I DON'T BELIEVE IT! YOU BROKE IN HERE LIKE THE SAFE WAS MADE OUT OF BUTTER!
BROTHER GRIMM HAS HIS WAYS, CONGRESSMAN.
NOW--THE MONEY!

ALL RIGHT, ALL RIGHT! I'LL GET IT. HOLD ON.
HURRY, CONGRESSMAN. I AM NOT A PATIENT MAN!

HERE'S YOUR MONEY, NOW PLEASE--GET ME HOME.
IT'S COLD IN HERE.
THAT IS YOUR PROBLEM, CONGRESSMAN -- NOT MINE. YOU SEE, FRIEND-- I HAVE YOUR MONEY...

...WHILE YOU, CONGRESSMAN, HAVE NOTHING!
SLAM

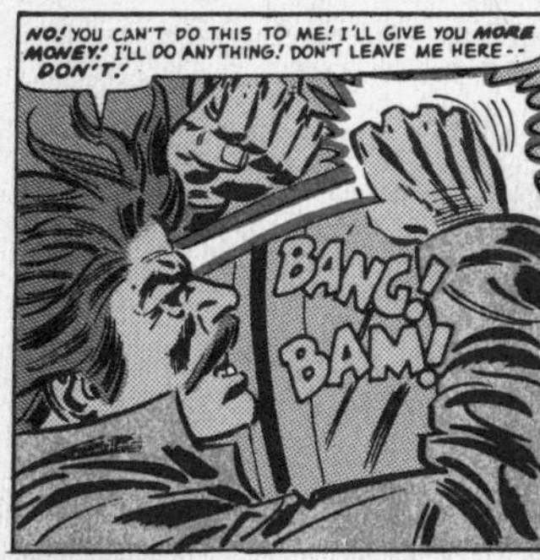
NO! YOU CAN'T DO THIS TO ME! I'LL GIVE YOU MORE MONEY! I'LL DO ANYTHING! DON'T LEAVE ME HERE-- DON'T!
BANG!
BAM!

EARLY THE NEXT MORNING IN A SMALL PARK...
TWO BEDROOMS, LIVING AND DINING ROOM. ONLY $340 A MONTH.
MAGNUS, I DON'T THINK WE'LL FIND AN APARTMENT WE CAN AFFORD.
CONGRESSMAN WYATT FOUND IN BANK VAULT
NONSENSE, MY DEAR, I ALREADY KNOW OF ONE.

REALLY? AND SINCE YOU ADMITTED YOU'VE NEVER BEEN TO L.A., AND SINCE I'VE BEEN DOING ALL THE NEWSPAPER CHECKING, JUST HOW DID YOU BECOME SO KNOWLEDGEABLE ABOUT ROOM VACANCIES?
JESSICA, MY DEAR, YOU STILL DON'T KNOW ME VERY WELL. COME WITH ME.
SOON...

WILL THAT DO, MY DEAR?
IT'S GORGEOUS. BUT ARE YOU SURE THEY'RE RENTING ROOMS? AND FOR HOW MUCH?

MY DEAR, SWEET INNOCENT--YOURS IS TO LOOK LOVELY IN THE FACE OF DANGER--MINE IS TO PERFORM MINOR MIRACLES, IF YOU WILL.
WAIT HERE WHILE I SEEK OUT THE OWNER OF THIS LOVELY DOMICILE.

AND...
MISTER MAGNUS, I'M SURE YOU'LL FIND MY HOME SIMPLY PERFECT FOR YOU AND YOUR... NIECE DID YOU SAY?
YES, M'DEAR, MY NIECE--JESSICA. A LOVELY GIRL, THOUGH NOT NEARLY AS SOPHISTICATED AS YOURSELF.
MR. MAGNUS, I DO BELIEVE WE WILL GET ALONG JUST SPLENDIDLY. NOW PLEASE, COME IN. I'LL SHOW YOU TO YOUR ROOMS.

MRS. DOLLY...
PLEASE, CALL ME PRISCILLA, AND I DO HOPE TO MEET YOUR NIECE VERY SOON.

I'M SURE YOU WILL, PRISCILLA. I'M QUITE SURE YOU WILL.

THIS WILL BE YOUR ROOM, MR. MAGNUS. IT WAS MY DEAR, SWEET NATHAN'S DEN, REST HIS SOUL.
IT FEELS SO STRANGE RENTING OUT HIS ROOM, BUT SINCE HIS DEATH, MY SONS AND I CAN USE THE MONEY.
THIS WILL DO QUITE WELL, MY DEAR. NOW, I THINK I'LL FRESHEN UP, IF YOU DON'T MIND.

AS PRISCILLA DOLLY CLOSES THE DOOR BEHIND HER...
I'M YOUR NIECE? WHY DID YOU LIE, MAGNUS?
YOU HAVE MUCH TO LEARN, JESSICA.

OUR RELATIONSHIP IS TOO DIFFICULT TO EXPLAIN WITHOUT FORCING MISS DOLLY TO RAISE A SUSPICIOUS EYEBROW.
WHY? CANNOT A MAN AND A WOMAN SIMPLY BE FRIENDS-- COMPANIONS, AND NOTHING MORE?

I'VE LIVED A VERY LONG TIME, MY DEAR, AND I'VE LEARNED THINGS ARE NOT SO SIMPLE. SO, FOR THE PRESENT, YOU ARE MY NIECE.
IT WILL MAKE OUR LIVES MUCH EASIER TO LIVE.
THIS ALL CONFUSES ME, MAGNUS. I WAS TRAPPED IN WUNDAGORE FOR SO LONG I STILL DO NOT FULLY UNDERSTAND THE WAYS OF MAN...
...AND THOSE I DO UNDERSTAND-- I QUESTION.
BUT I GUESS IT IS ALL UNIMPORTANT. MY CONCERN IS LEARNING WHERE MY FATHER LIVES.

IN WHICH CASE, MY DEAR--WHY DON'T WE VISIT HIM NOW?
YOU KNOW--?
I DO.

A SHORT TIME LATER...
OHH, MAGNUS--MAGNUS! YOU KNEW HE WAS DEAD ALL ALONG. WHY DIDN'T YOU TELL ME IN LONDON? WHY DID YOU HAVE TO BRING ME HERE? WHY?
YOU WOULD NOT HAVE BELIEVED ME, JESSICA-- I AM SORRY IF I DECEIVED YOU, BUT I THOUGHT IT WAS FOR THE BEST.

YOU DID, DID YOU? HOW DO YOU KNOW WHAT'S BEST FOR ME?
YOU TRICKED ME, MAGNUS-- LIKE THE HIGH EVOLUTIONARY DID--LIKE HYDRA TRIED TO.
DAMN IT, MAGNUS -- I'M NOT A PUPPET YOU CAN MANIPULATE WITH A STRING OF WORDS. I'M A HUMAN BEING... AND YOU TOYED WITH ME LIKE I WAS NOTHING.
NO, MY DEAR -- I WOULD NEVER PLAY GAMES WITH YOU. I SIMPLY THOUGHT YOU WOULD WANT TO LEARN WHO KILLED YOUR FATHER. THAT IS ALL.
WHAT?

LOS ANGELES GROWS DARK QUICKLY THIS NIGHT, DRAPING A SLIM, LITHE FIGURE IN DEEP, BLANKETING SHADOWS.
POLICE HEADQ
GRACEFULLY, LIKE A FEATHER CARRIED ALONG ON A BREEZE, SHE GLIDES TOWARD HER DESTINATION: THE LOS ANGELES POLICE DEPARTMENT...

INSIDE THE STONE BUILDING, SHE CAUTIOUSLY ADHERES TO CEILINGS-- AVOIDING THE SIGHT OF MEN AND WOMEN WHO PROWL THE CORRIDORS.

THIS IS THE RECORDS ROOM. WITH LUCK I'LL FIND WHAT I NEED.

D FOR DREW. HERE IT IS-- "JONATHAN DREW. MURDER UNSOLVED. INVESTIGATIONS STILL PENDING. J.R. BULLIT, DETECTIVE."
DREW
D-F
LET'S SEE WHAT THE REPORT SHOWS, THEN I JUST MAY SPEAK WITH MR. BULLIT, DETECTIVE.

EH--? NOISES IN THE NEXT ROOM. PEOPLE. COMING MY WAY?
WILL THEY DISCOVER ME HERE?
BLAST! I WANTED TO BE IN AND OUT OF HERE BEFORE THEY KNEW ANYTHING.
I WAS DETERMINED TO KEEP SPIDER-WOMAN'S PRESENCE IN THIS CITY A SECRET IF I COULD.

WHEW! THEY'RE STAYING IN THE NEXT OFFICE. BUT--WHAT ARE THEY SAYING?
...I KNOW THAT, CONGRESSMAN WYATT. MY MEN INVESTIGATED THAT LOONEY WHO HIT THE PLAYHOUSE LAST NIGHT.

WE'VE A HUNDRED WITNESSES WHO INSIST HE WAS A RAVING, RANTING WILD MAN. BUT NOW YOU SAY--
I SAY HE WAS COLD, SHREWD--VERY CALCULATING. NO OTHER KIND COULD HAVE MADE IT THROUGH MY ALARM SYSTEMS AND BROKEN INTO THE BANK SO EASILY.

GREAT--GREAT! JUST WHAT WE NEED... A SCHIZOID LOONEY-TOON
WHY, LORD--WHY COULDN'T YOU SEND HIM TO SOME OTHER DISTRICT--PREFERABLY IN COLORADO?!

THEY HAVE THEIR WORRIES, I HAVE MINE! BUT I'VE GOT WHAT I CAME FOR--
--AND WITH LUCK THE PAPERS WILL SUPPLY SOME CLUE TO MY FATHER'S MURDERER.

HOME, A FEW MINUTES LATER...
ANYTHING OF IMPORT, JESSICA?
PRECIOUS LITTLE. JUST THAT HE WAS KILLED TWO MONTHS AGO... THAT HE WORKED FOR SOME OUTFIT CALLED PYRO-TECHNICS, AND--WAIT!
CURIOUS! HE HAD A RUN-IN WITH A CONGRESSMAN WYATT. WYATT WAS AT POLICE HEADQUARTERS WHILE I WAS, UH--VISITING THERE.

SOMETHING TELLS ME THIS SHOULD BE LOOKED INTO!
LISTEN, JESSICA-- SQUABBLING FROM DOWNSTAIRS.

EH--? COME HERE, MAGNUS-- THEY MUST MUST BE PRISCILLA DOLLY'S OFFSPRING.

JUST FORGET IT, WILLIAM. I'M NOT INTERESTED IN YOUR TROUBLES.
YEAH? WELL, YOU'RE GONNA BE CONCERNED PRETTY SOON, BROTHER. I'LL MAKE SURE OF THAT.

NOW, NOW--PLEASE, BOYS--NO FIGHTING! OH, WHY CAN'T WE HAVE A PEACEFUL HOME...LIKE BEFORE YOUR FATHER PASSED ON?
IT WAS JAKE'S FAULT, MOM.
IF THERE'S ANYTHING WE HATE, IT'S GETTING INVOLVED IN A FAMILY FEUD. SO, LET US CUT TO THE NEXT DAY... AND THE CAPITOL BUILDING.
CONGRESSMAN WYATT?

HUNH? WHO IN BLAZES ARE YOU? HOW DID YOU GET IN HERE?
GUARDS!
MY NAME IS UNIMPORTANT, CONGRESSMAN. BUT I'VE QUESTIONS FOR YOU TO ANSWER.

LISTEN, LADY, YOU'RE ON MY TURF. I DON'T ANSWER TERRORISTS' QUESTIONS--
--AND I'M SICK ALL THE WAY TO MY GUTS OF BEING PUSHED AROUND BY EVERY BLASTED WEIRDO IN A SKIN-TIGHT SHOW-OFF'S COSTUME!

DON'T DO IT, CONGRESSMAN.
ZZDAAK
WHAT? HOW DID YOU DO THAT?

JUST BE PLEASED I DIDN'T USE MY VENOM BLAST TO KILL.
ANSWER MY QUESTIONS, CONGRESSMAN--BEFORE I ALLOW MYSELF TO GET ROUGH.
JONATHAN DREW! WHAT HAPPENED TO HIM?

WHAA? THIS IS ALL ABOUT THAT CREEP? DREW WORKED FOR PYRO-TECHNICS... HE CAME TO SEE ME ABOUT SOME DISCOVERY HE MADE.
BUT HE WAS JUST SOME EGG-HEADED PEST, SO I GOT MY GUARDS TO SHOO HIM AWAY.

I--I DON'T KNOW WHAT'S HAPPENED TO HIM SINCE--AND THE LAST I SAW HIM WAS ABOUT TWO MONTHS AGO.

WHY DID HE COME TO YOU? YOU'RE NOT A SCIENTIST!

BUT, JUST THEN...
KRAASH!
I'M BACK, WYATT! DID YOU TAKE ME FOR A FOOL?
WHAT? NOT AGAIN--NOO!!

WHO ARE YOU?
STAY OUT OF THIS, GIRL-- MY BUSINESS IS WITH THE CONGRESSMAN!
YOUR MONEY WAS COUNTERFEIT, CONGRESSMAN--AS PHONY AS YOU ARE. AND HERE I THOUGHT YOU WERE ONLY CHEATING YOUR CONSTITUENTS!

I WANT REAL CASH, WYATT--ONE HUNDRED THOUSAND DOLLARS' WORTH!
WAIT YOUR TURN, MAN--I WAS HERE TO SEE WYATT FIRST!

I DON'T KNOW WHO YOU ARE, LADY--FRANKLY, I DON'T EVEN CARE.

BUT WHEN BROTHER GRIMM IS MADE OUT TO BE A FOOL--
WHAK!

--ANYONE WHO STEPS IN HIS WAY-- SUFFERS!
AND I DO MEAN EVERYONE!

INCLUDING FANCY-DRESSED FEMALES!

WRONG, SKULL-FACE. YOU HAVEN'T HALF THE NECESSARY STRENGTH TO STOP ME.
WHAP!

MEANWHILE...
YOU HEARD ME, FOOL -- GET THE COPS HERE--ON THE DOUBLE!
DON'T ASK QUESTIONS, YOU BUMBLING SYCOPHANT -- MOVE!

STRENGTH ALONE IS NOT BROTHER GRIMM'S WAY, WOMAN--
I POSSESS THE UNCANNY ABILITY TO THINK AND ACT SIMULTANEOUSLY!
WITNESS HOW A COMMON TABLE LAMP CAN BECOME AN INSTRUMENT OF DEATH!
ZZZAKKK

A TRICK, SKULL-FACE... NOTHING MORE!
ZDAK!
WHAT?
AND THE SPIDER-WOMAN DOESN'T FALL FOR TRICKS!

NOW, CONGRESSMAN, SHALL WE START OVER AGAIN?
JONATHAN DREW-- TELL ME EVERYTHING ABOUT HIM!
AND FOR YOUR SAKE, LEAVE NOTHING OUT!

YOU'RE IN NO POSITION TO DEMAND ANYTHING. LISTEN--!
KREE SKREE SKREE
SIRENS? THE POLICE?
I GIVE YOU CREDIT, CONGRESSMAN-- FOR HAVING THE AUDACITY TO CALL THEM.

FAREWELL, FOR NOW. BUT I WILL BE BACK!
YOU'RE SCARING ME, LADY. YOU SHOW YOUR FACE AROUND HERE--
--AND I SWEAR YOU'LL BE A DEAD WOMAN!

SHORTLY AFTER...
HERE HE IS, OFFICER. THE SAME CREEP WHO ROBBED ME LAST NIGHT.
HE RETURNED FOR MORE MONEY!

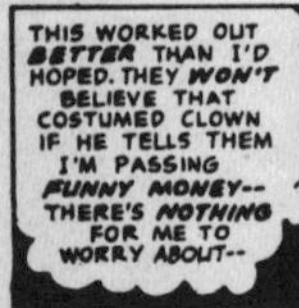

THIS WORKED OUT BETTER THAN I'D HOPED. THEY WON'T BELIEVE THAT COSTUMED CLOWN IF HE TELLS THEM I'M PASSING FUNNY MONEY-- THERE'S NOTHING FOR ME TO WORRY ABOUT--
--EXCEPT FOR THAT STRANGE WOMAN. SHE OVERHEARD GRIMM... SHE KNOWS MY SECRET.
WELL, SHE'S THE ONE WHO'D BETTER WORRY. I'VE GOT THE FULL POWER OF THE GOVERNMENT BACKING ME UP--AND THAT'S ENOUGH TO FIND THE LITTLE TRAMP--
--AND TO SILENCE HER... BEFORE SHE CAN RUIN ME!

A DAY GOES BY, AND THEN NIGHT ONCE AGAIN HOLDS LOS ANGELES IN ITS EBON HANDS...
BLAST! WYATT'S GOT HIMSELF SURROUNDED BY FLUNKIES... NO WAY TO GET TO HIM ALONE.
HE'S MIXED UP WITH SOMETHING CROOKED, BUT I DON'T KNOW IF IT HAS ANYTHING TO WITH MY FATHER'S DEATH.
I'M CHECKMATED HERE... BUT I'VE ONE OTHER CLUE... PYRO-TECHNICS, INC.

BUT FIRST-- POLICE H.Q.
THIS FRIGHT-MASK MUST BE GLUED ON. IT WON'T COME OFF.
IT IS CHEMICALLY SET IN PLACE, FOOL. ONLY BROTHER GRIMM CAN REMOVE IT!

YEAH? WELL, WE'LL GET IT OFF EVEN IF WE GOTTA PRY IT LOOSE WITH A CROW BAR!

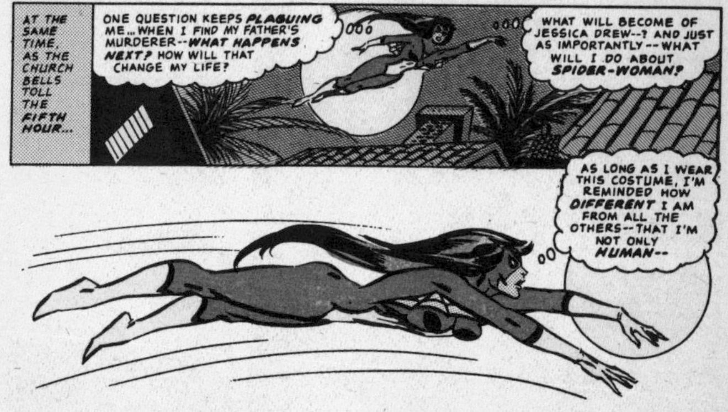
AT THE SAME TIME, AS THE CHURCH BELLS TOLL THE FIFTH HOUR...
ONE QUESTION KEEPS PLAGUING ME... WHEN I FIND MY FATHER'S MURDERER--WHAT HAPPENS NEXT? HOW WILL THAT CHANGE MY LIFE?
WHAT WILL BECOME OF JESSICA DREW--? AND JUST AS IMPORTANTLY--WHAT WILL I DO ABOUT SPIDER-WOMAN?
AS LONG AS I WEAR THIS COSTUME, I'M REMINDED HOW DIFFERENT I AM FROM ALL THE OTHERS--THAT I'M NOT ONLY HUMAN--

--BUT I'VE GOT THE BLOOD OF A SPIDER COURSING THROUGH MY VEINS! WAIT-- SOMETHING--?
GAS!

CAN'T CONCENTRATE... CAN'T KEEP AFLOAT... FALLING...

GRIMM? I THOUGHT THE POLICE CARTED YOU AWAY? HOW?
HEE HEE HEE! THAT'S FOR ME TO KNOW, YOU LITTLE TWIT-- AND FOR YOU TO UNCOVER!

OH, LET ME GIVE YOU A HAND IN GETTING UP!
WHAT--? IT CAME LOOSE!
OF COURSE IT DID, YOU NINNY! YOU SEE, I'M A TRICKY LITTLE DEVIL--

WHAT IS THIS? THE HAND EXPLODED!
BAMM!

DON'T WORRY, GIRLY, 'TWAS ONLY A SMALL EXPLOSIVE--
YOU SEE, I DON'T WANT TO BOMB YOU OUT ON OUR FIRST DATE!

SO LET IT SERVE AS WARNING, FRILL--GET LOST! BUZZ OFF. IN UDDER WORDS, KIDDO--SCRAMAYVOO!
TOODLE-OO, GORGEOUS!
GRIMM ESCAPING ON A CLOUD? IT DOESN'T MAKE ANY SENSE!

YOU MAY HAVE ESCAPED THE POLICE, GRIMM--BUT YOU'RE NOT ESCAPING ME!
AH, YER GIVIN' CHASE TA OLE B.G., ARE YA, LASSIE? THEN LET THIS SON A' OLE ERIN GIVE YE SOMETHIN' IN TURN.
MY SPECIALLY PATENTED FULLY GUARANTEED GRIMM-BOMB!
COMPLIMENTS A' YE BROTHER, ME LASS.

IT IS ESPECIALLY USEFUL IN STOPPING BUNNY RABBITS, TIMBER WOLVES, AND MEDDLESOME FLYING FEMALES!
ONCE MORE--TA TA!

GONE--AS IF HE WERE NEVER HERE--
AND THAT LEAVES ME WITH NOWHERE TO GO.

AND SOON...
...NO CLUES, AND HE DELAYED ME UNTIL PYRO-TECHNICS CLOSED FOR THE DAY.
WHAT CAN I SAY BUT BETTER LUCK NEX--EH?
...AND THE RECENTLY APPREHENDED CRIMINAL CALLED BROTHER GRIMM--
--MYSTERIOUSLY ESCAPED FROM HIS PRISON CELL TODAY--AFTER THE SIX-THIRTY CELL CHECK. THERE ARE NO CLUES AS TO...
WHAT? HE ESCAPED AFTER SIX? BUT--I FOUGHT HIM AT FIVE O'CLOCK!
MAGNUS--TELL ME WHAT IS GOING ON? TELL ME!
YOU JUST MAY FIND OUT NEXT ISSUE!
RETURN OF THE HANGMAN!

Stan Lee PRESENTS: THE MYSTERIOUS SPIDER-WOMAN!

MARV WOLFMAN *WRITER / EDITOR* ✱ CARMINE INFANTINO *PENCILS* ✱ TONY DeZUNIGA *INKS* ✱ JOE ROSEN *LETTERER* ✱ MARY TITUS *COLORIST*

PERHAPS MY FUTURE WILL BE CLEARER ONCE I'VE DISCOVERED MY PAST. ONCE I'VE LEARNED WHO KILLED MY FATHER--
--THE MAN, WHO IN SAVING THE LIFE OF HIS BABY GIRL...
...CREATED THE MONSTER CALLED SPIDER-WOMAN.

MAYBE THEN I CAN REMOVE THIS COSTUME AND MASK--AND LET THE WOMAN WHO WEARS IT LIVE OUT HER LIFE--IN PEACE.
EH--? THAT CAR SPEEDING BELOW, AND ON ITS ROOF--
--BROTHER GRIMM ?!?

HA HAH! SO YOU THOUGHT YOU COULD ESCAPE OLE B.G., DID YA?
SHAME, SHAME--DON'T YOU KNOW I CARRY ALONG A GRIMM GRENADE JUST TO PREVENT THAT KIND OF THING?

TRA LA! AND ANOTHER DIAMOND MERCHANT IS DONE AWAY WITH, ALLOWING A POOR-BUT-HOPEFUL BROTHER GRIMM TO COLLECT THE SPARKLING GOODIES HE CARRIED WITH HIM.
WHAP

KRAK!
YOU WERE A FOOL TO SHOW YOUR SKULL-FACE IN PUBLIC, GRIMM.
DID YOU THINK SPIDER-WOMAN HAD FORGOTTEN WHO YOU ARE?
OH, PERISH THE THOUGHT, GIRLEE.

I WAS ITCHIN' FER ANOTHER MEET, MY FRILL...
WHAT?!?
...JUST SO I COULD GIVE YA MY SPECIAL GRIMM GIFT HORSE IN THE EYE!

I WASN'T PREPARED FOR THAT ELECTRIC BLAST!
BUT BROTHER GRIMM HAS RUN OUT OF HIS BAG OF TRICKS--!

GRIMM, THIS TIME WE--

--GONE? BUT IT ONLY TOOK MOMENTS TO PULL OUT OF MY FALL... TO GLIDE BACK TO THIS CLIFFTOP.
HOW COULD HE HAVE VANISHED SO QUICKLY? HOW?

BUT THAT IS A QUESTION NOT DESTINED TO BE ANSWERED. FOR NOW WE SWITCH TO...
STILL THINK WASTIN' DIAMONDS LIKE THIS IS A CRIME, NO MATTER WHAT THE BOSS SAYS.
BUT I AIN'T GONNA ARGUE WITH THAT SKULL-FACED FRUITCAKE.

HE SAYS, "LOOIE, TOSS THIS BAG A' DIAMONDS NEXT TO SOME JERK," I DO IT.
HE SAYS DOUSE THE JERK IN CHEAP BOOZE AN' RUN 'IM OFF A MOUNTAIN, I DO THAT, TOO.
LONG AS HE PAYS I DO WHAT HE SAYS.

I SEEN TOO MANY GUYS RUBBED OUT FOR ASKING LOONEYS LIKE HIM QUESTIONS. AN' I AIN'T PUTTIN' MY NECK ON THE--?!
FILTH! SCUM! CORRUPTER OF JUSTICE!

YOU'VE COMMITTED YOUR LAST ACT OF VILLAINY, EVIL ONE!

BUT BEFORE I DEAL WITH YOU, I DEMAND ANSWERS!
THUMP!

JEWELRY MERCHANTS HAVE BEEN DISAPPEARING FOR WEEKS!
KAKK!

WHO IS THE EVIL FORCE BEHIND THESE ABDUCTIONS? WHO?
DON'T MAKE ME TELL YOU-- HE'LL KILL ME!
I AM HERE, VILLAIN. I AM YOUR IMMEDIATE THREAT. SPEAK!

GRIMM... HIS NAME'S GRIMM! HE'S KILLING THE DEALERS-- TAKIN' THE STONES.
BUT HE WANTED TA SWIFT THE BLAME-- HE HAD ME FIND THIS GUY HERE-- PLANT A COUPLE A' DIAMONDS WITH HIM SO THE COPS WOULD--!

ENOUGH! WHERE IS THIS GRIMM?
HE'S GOT HIMSELF A WARE-HOUSE-- ON FIFTH STREET. LOOK, I TOLD YOU EVERYTHIN' I KNOW. LET ME GO-- LET ME GO!
AND PERMIT YOU TO ROB AGAIN-- TO KILL ANOTHER INNO-CENT? DO YOU TAKE ME FOR A FOOL?

YOU SHALL DIE, EVIL ONE-- JUSTICE IS THE HANGMAN'S NOOSE!
AND JUSTICE SHALL BE SERVED-- TONIGHT!

THE FOOL EXPECTED LENIENCY.
AND WHAT ELSE SHOULD HE EXPECT-- IN A SOCIETY THAT CODDLES ITS CRIMI-NALS?
THE POLICE TURN THEIR BACKS ON CRIME! THE COURTS DISMISS EVIL-DOERS... RETURN THEM TO THE STREETS TO WREAK MORE HAVOC ON THE INNOCENTS WHO LIVE IN FEAR.

BUT THE GOOD NEED CRINGE NO MORE! THE LAW-ABIDING CITIZEN HAS FOUND HIS MASKED AVENGER TO HUNT HIS CRIMINALS DOWN--TO PUNISH ALL WHO COMMIT EVIL--
--AND TO PROTECT ALL WHO ARE INNOCENT.
THE HANGMAN LIVES--AND HE ACTS TO QUELL THE RAGE THAT DWELLS WITHIN US ALL!

ELSEWHERE...
I TOLD YOU, YOU LITTLE NINNY-- I GOT THE SPARKLERS! SO, NYAH-NYAHH!
WHATTAYA LOOKIN' AT ME LIKE THAT FOR? THERE'S ENOUGH--YOU THINK I'D LEAVE ALL THAT LUSCIOUS LOOT BEHIND AT THE PLAY-HOUSE IF I HADN'T COME UP WITH A BETTER SCHEME?

OH, POOH--I'M RICHER THAN YOU, AND YOU'RE JUST JEALOUS, THAT'S ALL.
AFTER ALL, ALL YOU DO IS SIT ON YOUR DUFF, WHILE I SKIP ALONG COLLECT-ING CASH AND OTHER GOODIES.

BUT YOU CAN'T BE BOTHERED WITH THAT, CAN YOU? YOU'RE TOO BUSY MAKING PRETTY AT ALL THE GIRLEES.
BAH! I'VE BETTER THINGS TO DO THAN WASTE MY TIME ON CHICKS.

SO, POOH ON YOU. I'LL LAUGH WHEN I'M A RICH MILLIONAIRE, AND YOU'RE NOT!
GO FLUSH YOURSELF DOWN A TOILET FOR ALL I CARE.

I'M GETTING OUT OF HERE -- THE AIR'S SO FOUL I FEEL LIKE I'M GONNA PUKE OUT MY GUTS.

SEEYA IN THE CARTOONS. TOODLES.

NORTH HOLLYWOOD, AND THE LOVELY FRAME HOME OF PRISCILLA DOLLY...
MAGNUS, I JUST LOVE YOUR NEW HAIRCUT. IT MAKES YOU LOOK SO DIS-TINGUISHED.
THANK YOU, MY DEAR -- I DO FEEL DAPPER WITH MY HAIR TRIMMED.

OH, BY THE WAY, MAGNUS, YOU'VE BEEN HERE A WHOLE DAY, AND I STILL HAVEN'T MET YOUR NIECE, JESSICA.
THE SOLUTION TO THIS LITTLE PROBLEM IS ON THE WAY.
I HEAR HER FOOTSTEPS NOW.

MRS. DOLLY, MY NIECE -- JESSICA DREW.
IT'S GOOD TO MEET YOU, MRS. DOLLY.
I FEEL SOMETHING STRANGE... THERE'S SOMETHING DIFFERENT ABOUT YOU -- SOMETHING I DON'T LIK--

NONSENSE, MY DEAR -- IT'S ONLY THE LIGHT, ISN'T IT, JESSICA? ISN'T IT -- PRISCILLA? JESSICA IS SUCH A SWEET, CHARMING GIRL. YOU MUST LIKE HER.
I... UHHH... I -- OHH, SHE IS SWEET, ISN'T SHE, MAGNUS -- EVERYTHING YOU SAID SHE'D BE.
I KNEW YOU'D SEE THINGS MY WAY, PRISCILLA.

THEN...
NO WAY, WILLIAM-- NO WAY!
WE'LL JUST SEE ABOUT THAT, JAKE.
YOU'LL COME AROUND. I--!

BOYS, NO SQUABBLING. PLEASE.
THESE ARE OUR NEW BOARDERS MR. MAGNUS AND HIS NIECE, JESSICA.

A MORE LOVELY ADDITION TO THIS HOUSEHOLD I CAN NOT IMAGINE.
I AM JAKE, AND YOU ARE AN ANGEL.
THANK YOU, JAKE. AND YOU MUST BE-- WILLIAM?

WILLIAM IS RATHER SHY, JESSICA. HE TAKES MORE AFTER HIS LATE FATHER, AND JAKE AFTER MY SIDE OF THE FAMILY.
JESSICA, DID MAGNUS SAY YOUR LAST NAME IS DREW?

YES. WHY--?
WE HAD SOMEONE STAYING HERE WHOSE NAME WAS DREW. WILLIAM, DIDN'T HE WORK WITH YOU--AT PYRO-TECHNICS?

UHHH, I--I DON'T REMEMBER, MOTHER.
OH, SURE YOU DO-- HE WAS A NICE MAN. HIS NAME WAS--OH YES, JONATHAN DREW.
MY FATHER?

JONATHAN DREW IS MY FATHER! HE'S THE REASON I'VE COME TO LOS ANGELES. PLEASE TELL ME WHAT YOU KNOW ABOUT HIM.
UHHH, NOTHING--NOTHING! HE WORKED AT PYRO FOR A FEW MONTHS, BUT IN SOME OTHER DIVISION.
HE WAS LOOKING FOR AN APARTMENT, SO WE BOARDED HIM HERE FOR A FEW WEEKS.
THAT'S ALL. THERE WAS NOTHING TO IT. WHY DO YOU WANT TO KNOW?

MY FATHER WAS MURDERED-- AND I AM SEARCHING FOR HIS KILLER!
MURDERED? OH, MY...

THIS IS THE SECOND TIME I'VE HEARD PYROTECHNICS MENTIONED. WILLIAM, I MUST SPEAK WITH YOU.

I'M SORRY, BUT I HAVEN'T THE TIME.
MOTHER, IF YOU'LL EXCUSE ME.
AND ME, MAGNUS. I'VE BUSINESS OF MY OWN.

YOUTH! ALWAYS RUSHING ABOUT SOMEPLACE OR ANOTHER.
MY DEAR, WOULD YOU PLEASE PASS THE POTATOES?
MURDER--? SUCH A HORRIBLE THING!

SHORTLY...
THERE IS SOMETHING WRONG ABOUT THIS PYRO-TECHNICS BUSINESS... SOMETHING I'D BEST INVESTIGATE.
AND I STILL WANT TO LEARN THE CONNECTION BETWEEN MY FATHER-- AND CONGRESS-MAN WYATT!

WHICH IS AS PERFECT A SEGUE AS POSSIBLE TO LOOK IN ON OUR ERSTWHILE CONGRESSMAN...AND HIS WIFE.
I KNOW THERE'S POTENTIAL DANGER, BUT I'M JUST NOT SURE IF-- HOLD IT! GLORIA JUST WALKED IN.
ARE WE GOING SOMEWHERE TONIGHT, DEAR? YOU'RE DRESSED UP FOR A--
NOT WE, DARLING--I. I'VE GOT A LATE NIGHT DINNER WITH FRANK AND DINO.

OH, TAKE THAT POUT OFF YOUR FACE, LOVE--AND PLEASE DON'T COMPLAIN.
GLORIA, YOU'VE BEEN OUT EVERY NIGHT THIS MONTH. I THOUGHT WE'D STAY HOME TO-GETHER TONIGHT.

OH, JAMES, PLEASE DON'T BE SUCH A DRAG. I'VE MY FRIENDS, AND YOU'VE... YOURS.
BE A GOOD BOY, WILL YOU? BYE.
YEAH-- GOOD-BYE.

FURS... NEW GUCCI SHOES AND BAGS EVERY WEEK. SHE SPENDS MY MONEY LIKE IT'S GOING OUT OF FASHION.
NO WONDER I'VE BEEN FORCED TO MAKE DEALS WITH--
OH--YES, I'M STILL HERE. LOOK, I'LL LEAVE IT IN YOUR HANDS--DO WHAT YOU MUST-- BUT GET SPIDER-WOMAN OUT OF MY HAIR--FOREVER!

LOS ANGELES INTERNATIONAL AIRPORT...
AHHH, YOU MUST BE JERRY HUNT. I'M BILL FOSTER.
MY BOSS, TONY STARK-- ASKED ME TO PICK YOU UP.
THANKS, BILL-- I WAS WONDERING IF SHIELD SET UP ANYTHING FOR ME.
TO ALL PASSEN

BILL, EVER SEE THIS LITTLE LADY? SHE'S THE ONE I'M LOOKING FOR.
HEY, NICE LOOKIN', BUT--NAHH! NOBODY AROUND HERE LOOKS LIKE THAT!
AND IF ANYONE WOULD KNOW, I'M THE MAN. I'M SORT OF AN EXPERT WHEN IT COMES TO COSTUMED CHARACTERS.

REALLY? WHAT DO YOU DO FOR STARK? PINCH HIT AS HIS BODY-GUARD WHEN IRON MAN IS AWAY?
NAH, I HEAD UP HIS RESEARCH UNIT OUT HERE, BUT HE ASKED ME TO DO HIM A FAVOR...
YOU KNOW, HE WORKS WITH SHIELD... AND YOU BEING AN AGENT--

HEY, YOU MUST BE STARVED. LOOK, I KNOW THIS LITTLE MEXICAN PLACE THAT'S GUARANTEED TO BURN OUT YOUR INSIDES. LET ME TAKE YOU THERE.
SOUNDS GOOD TO ME, MR. FOSTER. LET'S GO!

MEANWHILE...
EVERYTHING POINTS TO PYRO-TECHNICS... MY FATHER WORKED HERE-- WYATT HINTED SOMETHING WAS AMISS... EVEN WILLIAM'S SUDDEN NERVOUSNESS WHEN JONATHAN DREW'S NAME WAS MENTIONED.
PYRO-TECH
SPEAKING OF WILLIAM -- HIS CAR'S PARKED HERE. HE'S INSIDE.

WELL, IF HE'S INVOLVED WITH MY FATHER'S DEATH, THE BEST THING I CAN DO IS FOLLOW HIM... LEARN WHAT HE'S UP TO.

HUNH? HE'S GONE. THERE MUST BE SOME OTHER WAY OUT OF THIS WIND TUNNEL.

DOOR SLAMMING SHUT BEHIND ME...?
SLAMM!
SORRY, WILLIAM, BUT YOU'LL HAVE TO DO BETTER THAN THIS TO HOLD BACK SPIDER-WOMAN.

THERE ISN'T A DOOR MADE THAT CAN--
--GOOD LORD! HE'S STARTED UP THE EXHAUST FAN! IT'S SUCKING ME IN TOWARD THE BLADES!
WHIRRR
THE SUCTION'S TOO POWERFUL... I--I CAN'T BREAK FREE!

WHILE SPIDER-WOMAN BEGINS A DESPERATE STRUGGLE, WE MUST DETOUR EASTWARD TO A DARK, SECLUDED WAREHOUSE ON FIFTH STREET...
TWO HOURS...TWO MORE BLASTED HOURS, THEN WE SET THIS CREEP FREE!
THE DIAMONDS ARE READY?
THEY WILL BE BY THEN. THE BOSS SAID HE'D BRING THEM HERE IN ABOUT AN HOUR.

GOOD THING, TOO-- I CAN'T WAIT TO GET THIS CRAZY CAPER OVER WI-- AGGHHH!
THUNK!
F-FRANK?

JUSTICE IS NOW SERVED-- WITH THE DEATH OF A FIEND.
WHAM

HEY! YOU DON'T HAVE THE RIGHT TO--!
YOU DARE SPEAK OF RIGHTS WHEN YOU STEAL THE RIGHTS FROM OTHERS?
YOU HAVE NO RIGHTS, FILTH-- YOU HAVE NOTHING-- NOT EVEN YOUR LIFE... UNLESS YOU TELL ME WHAT I MUST KNOW.
A--ALL RIGHT...ALL RIGHT! I'LL TALK... JUST DON'T DO NOTHING.
I'LL TELL YOU EVERYTHING... ANYTHING YOU WANT ME TO TELL YOU.

AND, AT THAT SELFSAME MOMENT...
IT'S IMPOSSIBLE! THE AIR PRESSURE'S TOO STRONG! IT'S DRAGGING ME RIGHT TOWARD THOSE BLADES.
IF THESE STEEL SUPPORT STRUTS WEREN'T HERE, I'D BE LITTLE MORE THAN A MEMORY RIGHT NOW!
BUT--I'M NOT GIVING IN--THERE MUST BE SOME WAY TO--
SZAK!
WHIRRRR

MY VENOM BLAST! PERHAPS IT CAN--!
NO GOOD! IT CAN'T WORK AGAINST METAL-- ITS POISON ACTS ON THE HUMAN NERVOUS SYSTEM.

IN THAT CASE, THERE'S-- WAIT! I--I HAVE TO YANK LOOSE THIS STRUT-- IT'S MY ONLY CHANCE!
SNAPP!
I DID IT!

NOW, HAVE TO QUICKLY SPIN AROUND-- PUT THE STRUT BETWEEN THE BLADES AND ME--
KRUNCH!
--AND LET THEM CHEW ON SOME STEEL BEFORE IT HAS A CHANCE TO TOUCH MY SKIN!

IT WORKED-- THE BLADES SHATTERED.
NOW TO FIND WILLIAM-- LEARN WHY HE SET UP THIS TRAP, AND THEN--!
A-ALL OF A SUDDEN I'M GETTING THIS SICK IDEA THAT MAGNUS IS SOMEHOW INVOLVED.
IT CAN'T BE A COINCIDENCE THAT HE FOUND US ROOMS IN A HOME WHERE MY FATHER LIVED...
...OR THAT ONE OF THE SONS WHO LIVE THERE WORKED WITH MY FATHER JUST BEFORE HE WAS MURDERED.

COME TO THINK OF IT--MAGNUS SUGGESTED I CHECK THE POLICE FILES... AND IT WAS THERE I FIRST SAW CONGRESSMAN WYATT AND LEARNED HE KNEW MY FATHER AS WELL.*
HAVE I ALLIED MYSELF WITH A MAN WHO INTENDS TO MURDER ME?
WAIT-- OVER THERE!
*SHOWN LAST ISSUE.

WILLIAM DOLLY--I HAVE QUESTIONS FOR YOU TO ANSWER!
HUNH? WHO THE HECK ARE YOU? WHAT ARE YOU DOING HERE?

SHE HAS COME A LONG WAY TO FIND DEATH! HER DEATH!
WHAK!
THAT VOICE? IT CAN ONLY BE--

I HAVEN'T THE TIME FOR GAMES, GRIMM.
SZAK
NEITHER DO I, WOMAN! I'M HERE TO COMPLETE SOME UNFINISHED BUSINESS!
NAMELY-- YOUR DOOM!

HE SOUNDS SO DIFFERENT NOW-- HIS VOICE IS COLD... SELF-ASSURED. HE'S NO LONGER RANTING LIKE A MADMA-- WAIT!
THAT VIAL!
LADY, WE'VE GOT TO GET OUT OF HERE--
FWOOSHH

--IF THAT'S WHAT I THINK IT IS-- THIS LAB WILL BE A BLAZING INFERNO IN MINUTES. AND IF THE FIRE REACHES THE GENERATORS-- WE'LL BE BLOWN OFF THE MAP!
THEN RUN-- I'VE NO LONGER ANY REASON TO SPEAK WITH YOU.
IT'S OBVIOUS WILLIAM DIDN'T SET THE TRAP-- GRIMM DID.

WHAT ARE YOU WAITING FOR, WOMAN? AREN'T YOU GOING TO FOLLOW THAT QUAKING FOOL AS HE RACES FOR COVER?
OR DO YOU INTEND TO STAY BEHIND-- AND PERISH IN A FINAL BLAZE OF GLORY?!

I'M DOING NEITHER, BROTHER GRIMM!
I'M STAYING HERE JUST LONG ENOUGH TO CUT YOU DOWN--

--AND MAKE YOU ANSWER JUST A FEW SIMPLE QUESTIONS!
BROTHER GRIMM DOES NOT ANSWER QUESTIONS, WOMAN!

YOU CANNOT ANSWER QUESTIONS FROM THE GRAVE, VILLAIN!
AND THAT IS WHERE YOU SHALL SOON BE!
WHO--?

RELAX, WOMAN--I AM YOUR SAVIOR--I WILL GUARD YOU FROM THIS FIEND--AND PROTECT YOU FROM ALL EVIL.
WHAT ARE YOU DOING? WHO ARE YOU?

I AM JUSTICE UNCOMPROMISED BY FOOLS--AND I JUDGE YOU GUILTY OF CRIMES AGAINST MAN--
--AND I SENTENCE YOU TO DEATH!
YOU SEE, I'VE LEARNED YOUR SCHEME--HOW YOU CHEMICALLY REPRODUCED THE DIAMONDS YOU STOLE--HOW YOU GAVE THE COPIES BACK TO THE MERCHANTS THEN LET THEM GO FREE...
...WHILE YOU COVETED YOUR ILL-GAINED RICHES FOR YOUR OWN FIENDISH PURPOSES.
BUT NOW-- YOUR CRIMINAL DAYS ARE OVER-- FOREVER!
WHO ARE YOU? WHO ARE YOU?

SPARRANG!
I HAVE ALREADY TOLD YOU--I AM YOUR PROTECTOR! WOMEN ARE WEAK, FRAIL CREATURES--EASY PREY FOR THE DEPRAVED MINDS WHO INHABIT OUR CITIES.

BUT YOU NEED FEAR THE WORLD NO LONGER! YOU SHALL BE SAFE IN THE HANGMAN'S DUNGEON--
--FOR THE REST OF YOUR LIFE!

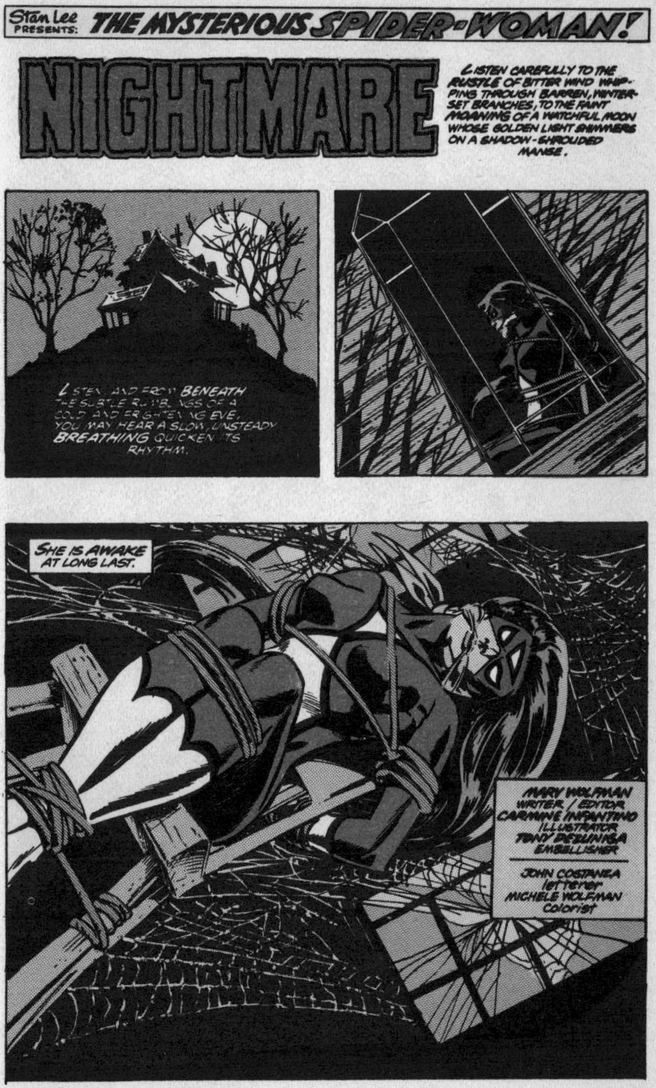

Stan Lee PRESENTS: THE MYSTERIOUS SPIDER-WOMAN!

NIGHTMARE

LISTEN CAREFULLY TO THE RUSTLE OF BITTER WIND WHIPPING THROUGH BARREN, WINTER-SET BRANCHES, TO THE FAINT MOANING OF A WATCHFUL MOON WHOSE GOLDEN LIGHT SHIMMERS ON A SHADOW-SHROUDED MANSE.

SHE IS AWAKE AT LONG LAST.

MARV WOLFMAN WRITER / EDITOR
CARMINE INFANTINO ILLUSTRATOR
TONY DEZUNIGA EMBELLISHER

JOHN COSTANZA letterer
MICHELE WOLFMAN Colorist

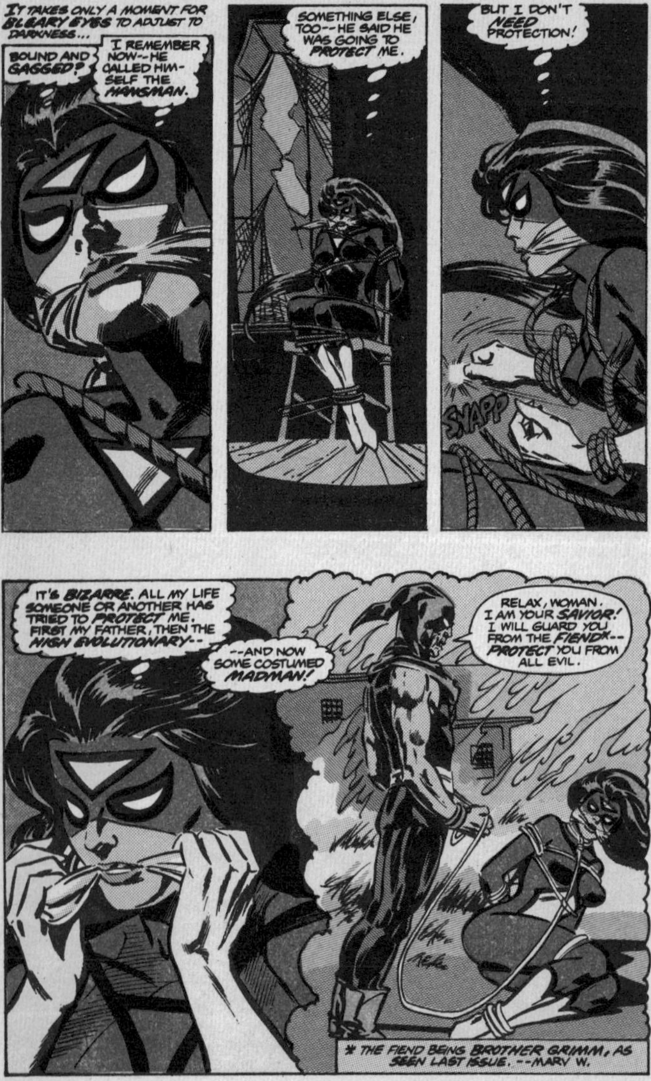

IT'S BIZARRE. ALL MY LIFE SOMEONE OR ANOTHER HAS TRIED TO PROTECT ME. FIRST MY FATHER, THEN THE HIGH EVOLUTIONARY--

--AND NOW SOME COSTUMED MADMAN!

RELAX, WOMAN. I AM YOUR SAVIOR! I WILL GUARD YOU FROM THE FIEND*--PROTECT YOU FROM ALL EVIL.

* THE FIEND BEING BROTHER GRIMM, AS SEEN LAST ISSUE. --MARV W.

UNDERSTAND THAT I AM JUSTICE UNCOMPROMISED BY FOOLS. YOU SEE, I UNDERSTAND HOW WEAK AND FRAIL WOMEN ARE.

YOU ARE EASY PREY FOR THE DEPRAVED MINDS WHO INHABIT OUR CITY.
BUT WOMEN NEED FEAR THE WORLD NO MORE. NOW THEY HAVE THEIR PROTECTOR IN THE GUISE OF THE AVENGING HANGMAN!

I SHALL SEE TO YOUR SAFETY BY KEEPING YOU IN MY DUNGEON--
--FOR THE REST OF YOUR NATURAL LIFE!

WHY DO YOU STILL STRUGGLE? DON'T YOU UNDERSTAND THAT I'M NOT YOUR ENEMY?

SOCIETY TORTURES YOU, THE LAW IGNORES YOUR CRIES. ONLY I STAND IN THE WILDERNESS, A BEACON OF LIGHT DEDICATED TO THE FUNDAMENTALS OF UNADULTERATED JUSTICE!
AND YOU POOR WOMEN ARE MERE BLIND SHEEP WHO MUST BE LED BY THE SHEPHERD OF RIGHTEOUSNESS.

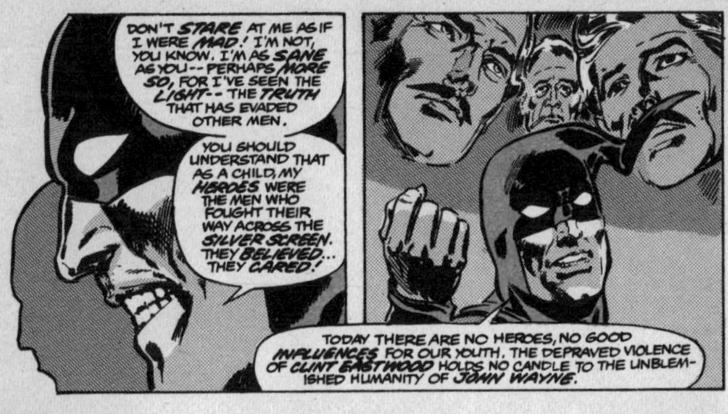
DON'T STARE AT ME AS IF I WERE MAD! I'M NOT, YOU KNOW. I'M AS SANE AS YOU--PERHAPS MORE SO, FOR I'VE SEEN THE LIGHT--THE TRUTH THAT HAS EVADED OTHER MEN.
YOU SHOULD UNDERSTAND THAT AS A CHILD, MY HEROES WERE THE MEN WHO FOUGHT THEIR WAY ACROSS THE SILVER SCREEN. THEY BELIEVED... THEY CARED!
TODAY THERE ARE NO HEROES, NO GOOD INFLUENCES FOR OUR YOUTH. THE DEPRAVED VIOLENCE OF CLINT EASTWOOD HOLDS NO CANDLE TO THE UNBLEMISHED HUMANITY OF JOHN WAYNE.

THE WORLD TODAY NEEDS A HERO--AND THE HANGMAN SHALL BE HE!
HERO? AN INSANE PSYCHOPATH IS MORE LIKE IT.
HE'S A MADMAN WHO BROUGHT ME TO THIS ROTTING HOLE THEN LEFT ME TO DIE WHILE HE RETURNS TO LOS ANGELES, PROBABLY TO FIND MORE WOMEN FOR HIM TO "PROTECT."

WELL, HE'LL FIND I'M NOT SO HELPLESS AS BEFORE. MY STRENGTH'S RETURNED, AND I-- EH?
SPIDERWEBS STRETCHED ACROSS THE CEILING? STRANGE, I HADN'T NOTICED THEM BEFORE.

SPIDERWEBS FOR A SPIDER-WOMAN. ALMOST APPROPRIATE, FOR I'VE THE BLOOD OF THE SPIDER COURSING THROUGH MY VEINS...
...AND THAT BLOOD MAKES ME LESS THAN BOTH THE SPIDER AND THE WOMAN I AM.

BUT SUDDENLY, THE GLISTENING WEBS ARE GONE, AND THE REFLECTION OF SPIDER-WOMAN SHIMMERS AND REFORMS, UNTIL...

AS IF IN ANSWER TO THE AMAZING HUMAN ARACHNID'S QUESTION, THE CEILING MIRROR SHATTERS INTO A THOUSAND GLEAMING AND GLISTENING SHARDS OF DEATH.

ROOTED BY SHOCK, SPIDER-WOMAN CANNOT MOVE, YET UNCONSCIOUSLY, SHE COUNTS OFF THE MILI-SECONDS REMAINING BEFORE THE SILVER-COATED SPEARS SLICE--THROUGH HER?

A SCRAPING WHINE FROM BEHIND IS ALL THE WARNING SPIDER-WOMAN HAS. BUT BY NOW, SHE IS PREPARED, AND INSTANTLY, SHE MOVES.
WHOMP
ALL RIGHT, NOW I KNOW... THERE'S SOMEONE HERE WITH ME... SOMEONE TRYING TO KILL OR CONFUSE OR DO SOMETHING WITH ME.
BUT WHY-- AND WHOM?
CERTAINLY THIS CAN'T BE THE HANGMAN'S DOI-- A SOUND ABOVE ME?

LORD, NOW THE CHANDELIER'S DROPPING!
WHOEVER IS BEHIND THIS IS A PERSIS-TENT DEVIL!
KRASH!

UNLESS IT'S THE HOUSE ITSELF...?
CALM DOWN, GIRL. HOUSES CAN'T BE POSSESSED. THAT'S FICTION FOR THE MOVIES. SUCH THINGS DON'T HAPPEN IN REAL-- WHAT?
WHAP
DAMN, I WASN'T PAYING ATTENTION. THAT HASSOCK FLEW ACROSS THE ROOM AT ME!

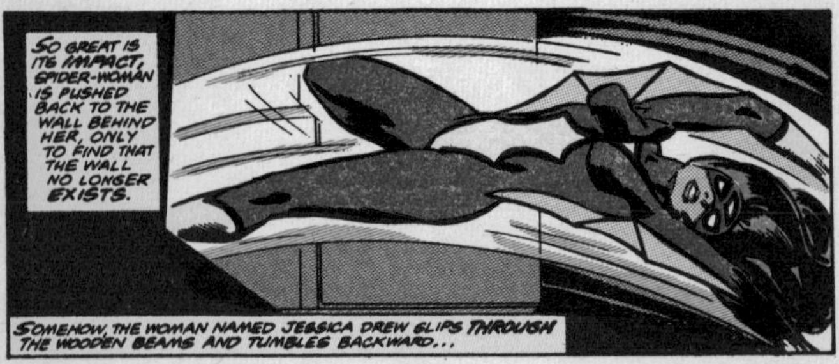
SO GREAT IS ITS IMPACT, SPIDER-WOMAN IS PUSHED BACK TO THE WALL BEHIND HER, ONLY TO FIND THAT THE WALL NO LONGER EXISTS.
SOMEHOW, THE WOMAN NAMED JESSICA DREW SLIPS THROUGH THE WOODEN BEAMS AND TUMBLES BACKWARD...

...INTO DARKNESS.
HERE, THERE IS NOTHINGNESS. NO SOUND, NO MOVEMENT, ONLY A VERY PUZZLED YOUNG WOMAN WHO FINDS HERSELF OUT OF CONTROL.
AS SHE HAS PREVIOUSLY STATED, ALL HER LIFE SOMEONE HAD PROTECTED HER. NOW, SHE REALIZES, SHE MUST FINALLY PROTECT HERSELF.

AND AS SOON AS THAT THOUGHT IS VERBALIZED, THE FALLING CEASES.
I'M CAUGHT IN SOME SORT OF GIANT WEB...
AND THAT MAKES MY PREDICAMENT ALL THE MORE LUDICROUS. THERE AREN'T ANY SPIDERS LARGE ENOUGH TO--EH?

A LIGHT? IT CAN'T BE A STAR, YET IT'S FLICKERING LIKE ONE.
NOW IT'S RE-SHAPING... INTO SOMETHING HUMAN!

LORD, I KNOW HIS FACE... THAT'S JERRY HUNT, THE POLICEMAN I MET IN LONDON.*
I'VE BEEN HUNTING FOR YOU, SPIDER-WOMAN!
SO, HE'S IN MY NIGHTMARE, TOO.
*SPIDER-WOMAN #1.--M.W.

AND NOW THAT I'VE FOUND YOU--YOU'RE GOING TO DIE!
NO, DON'T--STOP!
HE'S GONE! THEN THIS IS A NIGHTMARE. BUT I'VE NEVER HAD DREAMS LIKE THIS.
NOT EVEN IN WUNDAGORE.

WUNDAGORE? STRANGE THAT I SHOULD THINK OF THAT NOW. WUNDAGORE WAS SUPPOSED TO BE A PLACE WHERE DREAMS CAME TRUE. BUT FOR ME, WAS A NIGHTMARE!
ALL THE WHILE THE HIGH EVOLUTIONARY KEPT ME THERE, I WAS A DAMNED GUINEA PIG... JUST ANOTHER LABORATORY ANIMAL.
BUT I'M AN ANIMAL NO MORE. DO YOU HEAR THAT, HIGH EVOLUTIONARY--WHEREVER YOU MAY BE?

JESSICA DREW IS NOW A PERSON! A HUMAN BEING! DO YOU HEAR ME?
AND WHEREVER THE HIGH EVOLUTIONARY MAY BE, HE HEARS, AND HE SMILES.
AND SPIDER-WOMAN TILTS HER HEAD UP TO SEE A SHADOW DANCING IN THE NIGHT, A SHADOW THAT SLITHERS CLOSER... EVER CLOSER...

NORTH HOLLYWOOD, CALIFORNIA, AND THE HOME OF PRISCILLA DOLLY...
I MUST SAY, MR. MAGNUS, THAT I FIND YOU AND YOUR NIECE JUST FASCINATING.

AND, MY DEAR, YOU ARE A SHINING JEWEL IN A UNIVERSE OF DESPAIR. EH, WHAT IS THIS? AN EMPTY VASE?
HEAVEN FOREFEND!
SUCH A HAPPENSTANCE MUST NEVER AGAIN OCCUR!

FLOWERS? HOW DID YOU DO THAT, MR. MAGNUS?
POOF!
NOW, NOW, MY DEAR. A MAGICIAN NEVER REVEALS HIS SECRETS.

YOU'RE A MAGICIAN? HOW WONDER-FUL!
MAGIC IS SO FASCINATING. DID YOU SEE THAT DOUG HENNING ON THE TV? HE'S SO GOOD. TEA?
YES, THANK YOU.

MR. MAGNUS, IT'S SUCH A RELIEF HAVING A MAN HERE AGAIN. EVER SINCE MY DEAR NATHAN DIED, THIS OLD PLACE HAS BEEN SO LONELY.

WILLIAM AND JAKE ARE HARDLY EVER HOME, AND WHEN THEY ARE, THEY QUARREL ALL THE TIME. IT WAS NEVER THAT WAY WITH NATHAN.
OH, THE DEAR MAN WOULD SIMPLY RAISE AN EYEBROW AND THEIR SQUABBLING WOULD END.
THE BOYS SO NEED A FATHER FIGURE TO LOOK UP TO.
WHAT DID NATHAN DO FOR A LIVING, MISS DOLLY? IF YOU DON'T MIND TALKING ABOUT HIM, THAT IS...
OH NO, MR. MAGNUS, I DON'T MIND. NATHAN WAS A BUSINESS-MAN, AND VERY GOOD AT IT, OR SO I'VE BEEN TOLD.

HE'D TRAVEL AROUND THE WORLD AND HE'D ALWAYS BE SURE TO SEND ME BACK A DOLL. AND I DO SO LOVE DOLLS.

THEY'RE SO PRETTY, SO FRAGILE. AND NOW I HAVE THEM TO RE-MEMBER NATHAN BY.

BUT, AS A HAIRY, PULSING FEELER BRUSHES OVER SPIDER-WOMAN, HER UNIVERSE BECOMES BLACK AS DEATH ITSELF.

UNTIL, IN THE FARTHEST DISTANCE, A FLICKERING CANDLE LUMENS A MOST FRIGHTENING SIGHT...

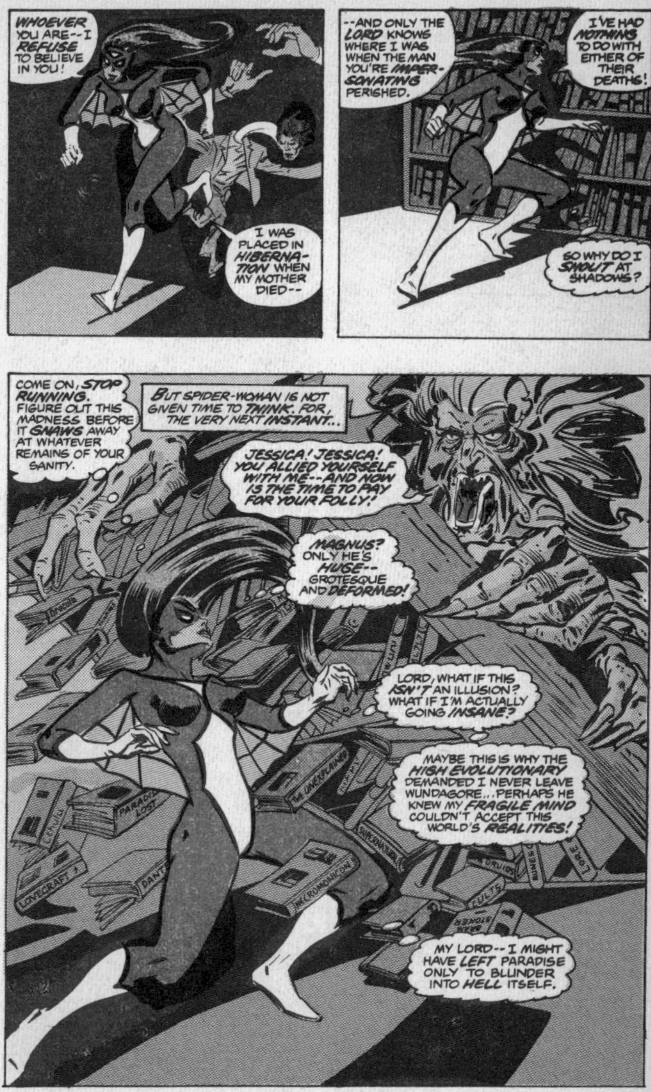

COME ON, STOP RUNNING. FIGURE OUT THIS MADNESS BEFORE IT GNAWS AWAY AT WHATEVER REMAINS OF YOUR SANITY.

BUT SPIDER-WOMAN IS NOT GIVEN TIME TO THINK. FOR, THE VERY NEXT INSTANT...

JESSICA! JESSICA! YOU ALLIED YOURSELF WITH ME--AND NOW IS THE TIME TO PAY FOR YOUR FOLLY!

MAGNUS? ONLY HE'S HUGE--GROTESQUE AND DEFORMED!

LORD, WHAT IF THIS ISN'T AN ILLUSION? WHAT IF I'M ACTUALLY GOING INSANE?

MAYBE THIS IS WHY THE HIGH EVOLUTIONARY DEMANDED I NEVER LEAVE WUNDAGORE... PERHAPS HE KNEW MY FRAGILE MIND COULDN'T ACCEPT THIS WORLD'S REALITIES!

MY LORD--I MIGHT HAVE LEFT PARADISE ONLY TO BLUNDER INTO HELL ITSELF.

NO, I MUSTN'T THINK THAT... I'VE GOT TO BELIEVE IN MYSELF. I KNOW I DIDN'T KILL MY PARENTS-- I KNOW THIS CAN'T BE MAGNUS LOOMING OVER ME.
BUT--WHETHER IT IS OR NOT-- IT CAN STILL KILL!
I'VE GOT TO FIGHT HIM! I'VE GOT TO WIN!

I'VE BEEN HUNTING FOR YOU, SPIDER-WOMAN!
AND NOW THAT I'VE FOUND YOU--YOU'RE GOING TO DIE!
LORD, HE'S STRONG--MY ARMS, MY LEGS, THEY'RE PINNED TO MY SIDE! I--!

WAIT--THOSE WORDS-- THEY'RE THE VERY SAME ONES JERRY HUNT SPOKE.
THEN THIS DEFINITELY ISN'T MAGNUS-- THIS HAS TO BE SOME INSANE GAME!
SOMEONE, SOMETHING--SOMEHOW --THIS HAS ALL BEEN ARRANGED SOLELY TO DRIVE SPIDER-WOMAN INSANE!
BUT I WON'T ALLOW IT! I WON'T! I WON'T!

SHE CALLS ALL HER INNERMOST POWER TO HER SELF, AND SUDDENLY THE OUTSIDE WORLD IS GONE. MAGNUS'S MONSTROUS SHOUTS FADE LIKE WHISPERS IN A WINTER'S WIND...

...AND ONCE MORE THE DARKNESS COMES AND PAINTS JESSICA'S WORLD IN BLACKS.

BUT EVENTUALLY...
I... I THINK IT'S OVER NOW. WHATEVER'S BEEN HAPPENING TO ME SEEMS TO BE ENDED.

NOTHING HERE BUT ME... THE TORCH--
--AND SOME ROTTING OLD STAIRS THAT WERE PROBABLY ANCIENT WHEN METHUSELAH WAS IN SWADDLING CLOTHES.

MUSTY OLD PLACE, LIKE SOMETHING OUT OF DANTE'S INFERNO-- & WAIT, THERE I GO AGAIN. I'VE NEVER READ DANTE, AND I'VE NEVER SEEN DORE'S ILLUSTRATIONS, YET HERE I AM COMPARING THEM TO THIS HOUSE--
--AS IF I KNEW WHAT I WAS TALKING ABOUT. YET, I DO-- SOMEHOW I KNOW WHAT THOSE ILLUSTRATIONS LOOK LIKE, SOMEHOW I KNOW WHAT THE INFERNO IS ALL ABOUT. BUT HOW--HOW?
BUT BEFORE THE AMAZING ARACHNID CAN PONDER HER QUESTION...

SO I'M NOT YET DONE WITH THE ILLUSIONS, AM I?
FROM THAT CASKET RISES A DRIED-UP CARCASS-- AND ONE WEARING MY SPIDER-WOMAN COSTUME.

ALL RIGHT, WHOEVER YOU ARE-- YOUR JOKE IS OVER.
WHAT?
STILL PLAYING GAMES, ARE YOU?

WHOEVER YOU ARE--YOU'RE A FOOL. DO YOU KNOW THAT?
IF YOU'RE TRYING TO KILL ME, YOU SHOULD HAVE DONE IT BEFORE THAT EPISODE WITH MAGNUS.

I ALMOST BELIEVED I WAS INSANE!
OH NO! VENOM BLAST IS USELESS AGAINST THEM.

NOW I KNOW THERE'S SOME-ONE OUT THERE--MANIPULATING THIS HOUSE INTO ATTACKING ME.
I KNOW IT, SO ANSWER, DAMN IT--ANSWER! WHERE ARE YOU?

SOMEHOW I DIDN'T EXPECT MY MYSTERIOUS ATTACKER TO SUDDENLY SPEAK UP. HE'S PLAYING HIS HAND RIGHT TO THE END.

HOPEFULLY NOT MY END, THOUGH.
WHOOSH!
EMPTY ANIMATED ARMOR... NOW WATER PIPES SET TO DROWN ME, MOST LIKELY.

A MIXTURE OF SORCERY AND CUNNING... WHO-EVER MY HIDDEN FOE IS, I'LL SAY ONE THING--HE COVERS ALL BASES.
AND HE'S CONFIDENT ENOUGH NOT TO TIP HIS HAND.

BUT WHY WORRY OVER WHO'S BEHIND THIS--
WHEN ALL MY ENERGIES ARE NEEDED TO ESCAPE THIS MADHOUSE?

GRASPING THE SWORD IN HER POWERFUL HANDS, SPIDER-WOMAN FORCES THE STEEL BLADE BE-TWEEN THE SLABS OF STONE THAT SURROUND HER.
AND SLOWLY, THE DARK ANGEL PRIES LOOSE THE FIRST MASSIVE ROCK.

THEN SUDDENLY, ONCE AGAIN, EVERYTHING IS GONE!
THE WATERWELL HAS VANISHED, ONLY TO BE REPLACED WITH THE FOUR WALLS OF THE HANG-MAN'S MANSION MACABRE...

IS THIS A STALEMATE, THEN? YOU'VE GIVEN UP TRYING TO DRIVE ME INSANE? DON'T YOU REALIZE YOU COULD NEVER GET MY PSYCHONEUR-OSES TO DESTROY ME?
WHOEVER YOU ARE--YOU'RE A FOOL! INSTEAD OF EXPLOITING MY WEAKNESSES, YOU'VE ONLY FORCED ME TO CONFRONT THEM.
AND NOW THAT I HAVE--THEY NO LONGER CAN HAUNT ME!
YOU'VE BLOWN IT! NOW YOU'VE NOTHING LEFT BUT TO REVEAL YOURSELF!

THERE IS NO ANSWER, SAVE FOR A SHIMMERING LIGHT THAT GROWS TO AN OVERWHELMING INTENSITY, AND THEN FADES, LEAVING BEHIND...

I AM MORGAN LE FAY... AND NOTHING THAT LIVES CAN STOP ME!
DOOM-SLAYERS! DESTROY THE FEMALE INSECT...
...WHILE I TAKE CARE OF THE MYSTERIOUS MAGNUS -- MYSELF!
NEXT ISSUE: AN INCREDIBLE COSMIC TOUR-DE-FORCE, AND CAUGHT DIRECTLY IN THE CENTER OF IT ALL: WEREWOLF BY NIGHT!

When young Jessica Drew was dying, her scientist-father injected her with a highly evolved serum of spider blood. The irradiated blood not only cured her, but changed her into the fearsome DARK ANGEL OF NIGHT.

Stan Lee PRESENTS: **THE MYSTERIOUS SPIDER-WOMAN!**

MARV WOLFMAN, WRITER • CARMINE INFANTINO, PENCILS • RICK BRYANT, INKS • J. COSTANZA, letters • BOB SHAREN, colors

PLEASE FORGIVE ME IF SOME OF WHAT I RELATE MAKES LITTLE SENSE. ALREADY MOST OF IT SEEMS LIKE A DREAM TO ME. A DREAM? PERHAPS I'D BEST CALL IT A-- NIGHTMARE.
YOU MAY AS WELL FOR-GET WHAT YOU'VE COME FOR, MORGAN --YOU'LL NEVER GET THE BOOK FROM ME.
I'VE FAILED IN THE PAST, BECAUSE OUR STRUGGLE WAS BETWEEN THE TWO OF US.

BUT NO MORE-- NO MORE!
THIS TIME A THIRD PARTY IS INVOLVED-- THIS TIME I SHALL STRIKE WHERE YOU ARE HELPLESS--

--THROUGH YOUR LOVE FOR ANOTHER!
MAGNUS, WHATEVER SHE WANTS-- REFUSE HER.
I CAN HANDLE MYSELF!
DON'T, JES-SICA--YOU CAN'T UNDERSTAND MORGAN...

SHE NEEDN'T UNDERSTAND ME, MY ONE-TIME LOVE-- SHE NEED ONLY FEAR THE SISTER OF ARTHUR.
SHE NEED ONLY DIE BY THE HAND OF MY HELL-SPAWNED DEMONS.
AND SHE WILL DIE, MAGNUS--UNLESS YOU STOP MY WARRIORS-- AS ONLY YOU ARE ABLE.
AND I TELL YOU AGAIN, WOMAN-- I CAN PROTECT MYSELF.
SWAK!

OH, SPIDER-WOMAN TRIED TO HOLD HER OWN...
...BUT IT WAS OBVIOUS FROM THE START, SHE WAS OVERPOWERED.
THE DEMONS LASHED OUT AT HER A DOZEN TIMES FOR EVERY BLOW SHE STRUCK.

NOT EVEN HER DEADLY VENOM-BLAST COULD STAY THE ETHEREAL CREATURES--HER POWERS WERE USELESS...

...AND MAGNUS KNEW HE COULD PERMIT THE STRUGGLE TO CONTINUE NO MORE.
MORGAN--STOP!
THE BOOK, MY LOVE--TELL ME WHERE TO FIND IT!

DAMN IT, MORGAN, MUST YOU MAKE ME GROVEL? STAY YOUR DEMONS, AND YOU'LL GET WHAT I'VE WITHHELD FROM YOU FOR ALL THESE CENTURIES.
AND I PRAY YOU CHOKE ON EVERY WORD.
YOUR PRAYERS MEAN NOTHING TO ME, MAGNUS.

JUST DISPATCH YOUR FEMALE--HAVE HER BRING THE BOOK TO ME.
MUST I, MAGNUS?
MY DEAR, PLEASE--GO. AND DO NOT WORRY.

EVEN AS MAGNUS NODDED IN SEEMING ACQUIESCENCE, A GOLDEN LIGHT SHIMMERED BRIGHTLY FOR A MOMENT ASIDE HIS TEMPLE, THEN VANISHED--

--ONLY TO REAPPEAR IN A SMALL, DARKLY-LIT ROOM IN THE LOWER CATACOMBS OF LOS ANGELES POLICE HEAD-QUARTERS--

--WHERE SHIELD AGENT JERRY HUNT TEDIOUSLY PORES THROUGH THE OFFICIAL MUG BOOK, IN SEARCH OF ANYONE WHO JUST MIGHT RE-SEMBLE THE TERRIBLY FRIGHT-ENED GIRL HE HAD BRIEFLY MET WEEKS BEFORE IN LONDON.

SHE CALLED HERSELF SPIDER-WOMAN...AND HE KNEW HER... FROM SOMEWHERE.

SUDDENLY, HIS EYES WENT BLANK, IF ONLY FOR AN INSTANT...

THEN, JUST AS SUDDENLY, HE SHOOK HIMSELF ALERT...
I'VE GOT TO GO.
YOU FOUND YOUR GAL?
UHHH, BEN--DON'T ASK ME HOW, BUT I KNOW WHERE SHE IS.
THE MUG BOOK HAS HER ADDRESS IN IT?
NO. I JUST KNOW.
LOOK, I'LL SEE YOU LATER.
SURE. GOOD LUCK, JERRY.

PLEASE DON'T ASK HOW I KNOW WHAT HAD ALREADY HAPPENED... I JUST DO...OR DID...
BUT AS MY MEMORY FADES, THE STORY FINALLY COMES 'ROUND TO WHERE I ENTERED THE SCENE. I, BEING MY HIRSUTE SELF.
SPIDER-WOMAN WAS FLOATING SOMEWHERE OUTSIDE COLDEN HOUSE, THE SINGLES' APARTMENT I PARKED MY BUTT IN.

LIKE A GENTLE STRAND OF GOSSAMER, SHE ALIGHTED ON THE SMOOTH POURED CONCRETE SHELL.
ONLY ONCE BEFORE HAD I WITNESSED SOMEONE WHO COULD ADHERE TO A BUILDING'S SIDE; HIS NAME WAS SPIDER-MAN... BUT HE WAS NOTHING LIKE THIS LITTLE LADY.
HE WAS BRASH, TALKATIVE, FLAMBOYANT.
SPIDER-WOMAN WAS SILENT, STALKING--SHE BECAME ONE WITH THE SHADOWS.
IN FACT, IF SHE HADN'T SPOKEN, I'D NEVER HAVE KNOWN SHE HAD SOMEHOW ENTERED MY APARTMENT TO FIND ME SHACKLED TO THE WALL. PANIC-STRICKEN, I SCREAMED...
GET OUT--WHOEVER YOU ARE--GET OUT!
I'M WARNING YOU--YOUR LIFE IS IN DANGER.
I AM HERE FOR YOU, JACK RUSSELL.

AND NOTHING, NOT EVEN THESE CHAINS, CAN KEEP YOU FROM ME.
WHO ARE YOU? WHAT DO YOU WANT?
OH NO--IT'S BEGINNING. LADY, PLEASE--FOR YOUR SAKE--GET OUTTA HERE!
GET OUT!!!

THEN IT HAPPENED, AS IT HAD EVERY MONTH SINCE MY EIGHTEENTH BIRTHDAY... THE FULL MOON WAS HIGH.
MY MIND BECAME CLOUDY, MY HEAD POUNDED IN AGONY. AND WITHOUT TOPAZ, THE MYSTERIOUS GIRL I LOVED, BESIDE ME, TEMPERING ME... I CHANGED...
THE CURSE OF THE WEREWOLF CONTROLLED ME ONCE MORE!

IT WAS MY FIRST NIGHT. TWICE MORE THIS MONTH THIS HIDEOUS MANIFESTATION WOULD OCCUR. I WAS A MINDLESS BRUTE SENSING ONLY AN ENEMY LURKING IN THE DARKNESS.
SAVAGELY, I LASHED OUT--

--ONLY TO DISCOVER MY PREY WOULD NOT BE EASY TO DEFEAT.

NEVER ONCE DID SHE EXPRESS SHOCK, OR TERROR. INSTEAD, SHE FOUGHT BACK WITH STRENGTH BELYING HER SLENDER FRAME.
THE BEAST I HAD BECOME WAS ENRAGED. THE HUMAN SHOULD HAVE FALLEN. YET, SHE STOOD DEFIANTLY, HOLDING HER OWN AGAINST MY SUPER-NATURAL POWERS.

INSANE, THE WERE-WOLF GRABBED HER TENDER NECK AND WITH ALL THE HIDEOUS EVIL POWER HE COULD CLAIM--
--HE STRANGLED THE GIRL, UNTIL SHE FELL UNCONSCIOUS TO THE GROUND.

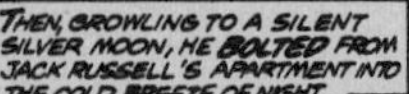
THEN, GROWLING TO A SILENT SILVER MOON, HE BOLTED FROM JACK RUSSELL'S APARTMENT INTO THE COLD BREEZE OF NIGHT.

IT WAS THE WEREWOLF'S NATURE TO SEEK FREEDOM, TO FIND A PLACE TO ROAM UNFETTERED FROM THE HARSH STENCH OF CIVILIZATION. THE FOREST, THE ONE AT THE EDGE OF TOWN, WOULD CALM HIS WILD RAGE...

...IF ONLY HE COULD REACH IT BEFORE DISASTER STRUCK.
WITHIN MY APARTMENT, SPIDER-WOMAN SHOVED THE COBWEBS FROM HER MIND. GROGGY, SHE ROSE BREATHING IN THE COLD NIGHT AIR. IT REFRESHED HER, INVIGORATED HER.
SO, JACK RUSSELL IS ALSO A WEREWOLF. WHY WASN'T I TOLD?
WELL, WHATEVER THE REASON, I MUST STILL SUBDUE HIM.

PERHAPS MY VENOM BLAST? IT WORKED ON LYCRUS WHEN HE AND I FOUGHT IN WUNDAGORE.*
*WUNDAGORE--THE CREATION OF THE HIGH EVOLUTIONARY WHO EVOLVED ANIMALS INTO ALMOST HUMAN INTELLIGENCE. LYCRUS WAS AN EVOLVED WOLF. --MARV.

BELOW HER ON THE STREET, MY WEREWOLF SELF SAW TWO EVIL EYES PIERCING THROUGH THE DARKNESS OF NIGHT--TWO HEADLIGHTS ON A SPEEDING CAR.
A CAR WHOSE DRIVER WAS SUDDENLY YANKED FROM HER PROTECTIVE COCOON.

GROWLING LIKE A RABID BEAST, HE *THRUST* THE WOMAN INTO THE AIR, UNSURE WHAT TO DO NEXT. FROM DEEP WITHIN HIM, I DESPERATELY TRIED TO *TEMPER* HIS BESTIAL URGES TOWARD VIOLENCE.

WHAT HAPPENED NEXT I CAN ONLY PIECE TOGETHER FROM THE MEMORY *FRAGMENTS* THAT STILL REMAIN. I WAS *UNCON-SCIOUS* AS THE CURIOUS MOB ENCIRCLED US...

A-ARE YOU *REAL*? ARE YOU?

ARE YOU *KIDDING*, ALICE? THIS HAS GOTTA BE FROM SOME *MOVIE*. IT'S *GOTTA* BE.

ARE YOU *MS. MARVEL*? I *HEARD* ABOUT YOU.

SHEESH, SHE'S NOT TALKING. SOME MOVIE STARS JUST GET *TOO BIG* FOR THEIR OWN GOOD.

...AND THEN, A MOMENT LATER, SHE GLIDED SKYWARD. BELOW US YOU COULD HEAR THE SHOCK OF THE DUMBSTRUCK CROWD.
SH-SHE'S FLYING... BUT I DON'T SEE ANY WIRES.
THEY WERE REAL! MY GOD, I'M GOING TO FAINT.

WITHIN THE AWESTRUCK CROWD, ONE MAN SMILED, THEN WALKED CALMLY TO HIS PARKED CAR.
HE HAD FOUND THE WOMAN HE HAD SEARCHED FOR, AND HE WOULD NOT ALLOW HER TO ESCAPE HIM AGAIN.

AS FOR ME, OR MY WERE-WOLF SELF, I WAS BROUGHT TO AN ANCIENT, CRUMBLING MANSE, STRAPPED STILL UN-CONSCIOUS TO A COLD, STEEL TABLE, WHILE THE WOMAN NAMED MORGAN LE FAY HOVERED VUL-TURE-LIKE ABOVE ME...
THIS CREATURE HAS THE BOOK? IF YOU ARE LYING TO ME, YOU'LL--
HE DOESN'T HAVE THE BOOK, MORGAN, BUT HE HAS READ THE DARKHOLD--AND ITS MEMORY STILL LINGERS IN HIS MIND.

THEN I SHALL SIMPLY REMOVE HIS MIND, GET WHAT I NEED, AND LEAVE HIM AN EMPTY HUSK.
NO!

AT LAST, I'VE FINALLY FORCED YOU TO WIELD YOUR FULL POWER.
NOW WE CAN FINALLY SETTLE WHICH OF US IS THE MORE POWERFUL--
--THE TEACHER--OR THE STUDENT!

MAGNUS MOVED SWIFTLY, HIS FINGERS CURLED THEN SPREAD WIDE, THEN SUDDENLY THE DARKENED ROOM WAS CAST IN AN EERIE, AMBER GLOW...
IS THAT YOUR BEST, MAGNUS? FOR SHAME--
--YOUR YEARS OF INACTIVITY HAVE WEAKENED YOU.

MORE THE SHAME, FOR I AM MORE POWERFUL THAN EVER!

MY DEAR, YOU MISTAKE A BEGINNING MOVE FOR A FINAL ATTACK. NOTHING COULD BE FARTHER FROM THE TRUTH.
HOW SHOULD I KNOW HOW MUCH ENERGY TO SUMMON WITHOUT FIRST TESTING YOU?
BEFUDDLED, SPIDER-WOMAN STOOD UNCERTAIN AMIDST THE GLOWING SPECTACLE. BEFORE HER, A MAN SHE THOUGHT SHE KNEW PERFORMED MIRACLES SHE COULD HARDLY BELIEVE.
I CAN ONLY IMAGINE WHAT WAS RACING THROUGH HER MIND AT THAT MOMENT.

BUT WHATEVER IT WAS, HER THOUGHTS MUST HAVE ENDED THE NEXT MOMENT, WHEN...
IT IS YOU... I HAD ALMOST LOST HOPE.
YOU? GET OUT OF HERE! IT'S TOO DANGEROUS!
NOT ON YOUR LIFE, GORGEOUS.

I'VE BEEN HUNTING YOU FOR WEEKS. I'M NOT GOING TO--WHA--?
WHAT IN THE WORLD IS GOING ON?
I--I DON'T THINK I COULD EX-PLAIN IT, NOT TO YOU... AND MAYBE NOT EVEN TO ME.

ONLY THING I'M SURE OF IS, SOMEHOW I'VE GOT TO HELP MAGNUS--
--ANY-WAY I CAN!
YOU LITTLE FOOL! YOUR POWERS CANNOT EFFECT THAT WHICH IS NOT TRULY THERE.
BUT STILL, I THANK YOU FOR REMIND-ING ME--

THERE IS MORE THAN ONE WAY TO DESTROY MAGNUS.
IF I CANNOT DESTROY HIS MAGIC, THEN I CAN DESTROY HIS FLESH!
FWISSSHH
SPINNING ABOUT, MORGAN'S FINGERS GLOWED SCARLET, THEN LIVING FLAME ERUPT-ED, CONSUMING THE HUMAN FORM OF MAGNUS...

WITHIN A MOMENT IT WAS OVER. WHERE THERE HAD BEEN LIFE, NOW THERE WAS ONLY CHARRED ASHES...
MAGNUS... DESTROYED?
MY FRIEND... DEAD?
NO... I CAN'T ACCEPT THAT. I REFUSE TO BELIEVE THAT!

MORGAN, FOR THE FIRST TIME IN MY LIFE, I WANT TO KILL!
STILL THE INSIGNIFICANT SNIT. HAVEN'T YOU YET REALIZED HOW POWER-LESS YOU ARE?
I'VE DESTROYED YOUR MEN-TOR. NOW I'LL RID MYSELF OF YOUR PRESENCE--BEFORE UTILIZING THE KNOWLEDGE THE DARKHOLD HAS GIVEN--

WHAT MADNESS IS THIS? A FIELD OF FORCE SURROUNDS YOU? HOW?

WELL, HOWEVER, IT WON'T MATTER--I'VE LEARNED ALL I NEED TO FROM THE DARKHOLD TO WEAVE A TIME-CASTING SPELL...

...TO FIND THE BODY OF MORGAN LYING UNCONSCIOUS IN HER ANCIENT CASTLE--AND TO AWAKEN HER.
WHEN YOUR FLESH TOUCHES MY ASTRAL SELF, WE SHALL BECOME ONE--

--AND WE SHALL RULE IN THIS CENTURY WHERE MAGIC HAS BEEN ALL BUT FORGOTTEN.
COME... COME--TOUCH ME, MORGAN--LET OUR FLESH AND SOUL MERGE ONCE AGAIN. LET US BE WHOLE!

NO! DAMN IT, I WON'T LET YOU SUCCEED.
MAGNUS WON'T HAVE DIED IN VAIN.
FEMALE, YOU ARE BECOMING TOO MUCH OF A PROBLEM.

I CAN NO LONGER AFFORD TO WASTE TIME ON YOU.
YOU MUST DIE-- NOW!

SHE STILL CAN'T HURT US. BUT HOW ARE YOU DOING IT, GORGEOUS?
FFFWISHHHH!
I DON'T KNOW-- I HAVEN'T ANYTHING TO DO WITH IT.
AND WHY DO YOU KEEP CALLING ME "GORGEOUS"? WHY HAVE YOU FOLLOWED ME HERE?
DON'T ASK ME TO EXPLAIN ANY OF THIS, BUT WHEN I SAW YOU IN LONDON * SOMETHING I DIDN'T KNOW WAS IN ME--STIRRED.
*ISSUE #1.--M.W.
THERE'S SOMETHING ABOUT YOU... SOMETHING THAT MAKES ME FEEL I KNOW YOU. SOMETHING THAT MAKES ME LOVE YOU!
LOVE? ARE YOU CRAZY, MAN? YOU DON'T EVEN KNOW WHO OR WHAT I AM.
LOOK, COMPLAIN TO WHOEVER SET UP MY GENE PATTERN.
ALL I KNOW IS WHEN I WAS RECOVERING IN THE HOSPITAL, I REALIZED THAT SOMEHOW YOU MEANT A HELLUVA LOT TO ME... MORE THAN ANYONE I HAD EVER KNOWN. I WANT TO KNOW YOU BETTER.

PROVIDING WE SURVIVE, THAT IS. ANY IDEAS, LITTLE LADY?
JUST ONE. MORGAN HINTED AT IT HER-SELF.
DISTRACT HER WHILE I PLAY OUT MY HAND.

NOW!
JERRY-- WATCH OUT!
YOU'VE LET DOWN THE FIELD? THEN YOU'VE PREPARED YOURSELF FOR DEATH!

YOUR WARNING COMES TOO LATE, FEMALE.
JERRY!
YOUR WOULD-BE LOVER IS DEAD!

THAT'S TWO DEATHS I OWE YOU FOR, MORGAN--
I'M EXTRACTING PAYMENT NOW!
WHAT? YOU'RE FIRING YOUR DAMNABLE VENOM BLAST AT MY REAL SELF! NO!

WHY NOT, MORGAN, ISN'T THAT WHAT YOU DID TO MAGNUS?
HAVEN'T YOU HEARD THAT TURNABOUT IS FAIR PLAY?

NO! MY FLESH IS DISINTERGRAT-ING!
I'LL DESTROY YOU FOR THIS, FEMALE!
I SWEAR...

...I'LL DESTROY...
...YOU... FOR... THIS...

THEN EVERYTHING WENT CRAZY. ALL THE LOOSE FURNITURE FLEW THROUGH THE ROOM TOWARD THE RIP IN TIME. IT WAS A MADDENING MAELSTROM FROM WHICH ABSOLUTELY NOTHING WAS SAFE.

SPIDER-WOMAN CLUNG TO THE TABLE I WAS STRAPPED TO, DETERMINED THAT AT LEAST WE WOULD NOT BE SUCKED THROUGH TIME AS WELL.

THEN, SUDDENLY, IT WAS ALL OVER--
KRAKOOOM!

--AND EVERYTHING THAT HAD BEEN. THE HOUSE, THE FURNISHINGS, EVERYTHING BUT THE HILL, SPIDER-WOMAN, AND ME, WERE GONE.
OR SO WE THOUGHT...
YOU'VE DONE WELL, JESSICA. YOU SHOULD BE PROUD OF YOURSELF.

MAGNUS? JERRY? BUT--?
I AM SORRY I HAD TO DECEIVE YOU, M'DEAR, BUT IT WAS NECESSARY TO LET MORGAN THINK SHE HAD DESTROYED US.

THE POOR WOMAN NEVER COULD BELIEVE I WAS MORE POWERFUL THAN SHE. I HAD TO PLAY ON HER EGO.
YOU CREATED THE FORCE FIELD, MAGNUS?
OF COURSE, M'DEAR, AND I MADE IT SEEM AS IF SHE REDUCED MR. HUNT AND I TO ASHES. BUT IT WAS YOU WHO DEFEATED MORGAN.

QUITE INGENIOUSLY, I MIGHT ADD. I NEVER WOULD HAVE THOUGHT OF IT. PERHAPS I'M GETTING OLD.
I DO KNOW I'VE EXPENDED THE VAST MAJORITY OF MY POWERS.

YOU SEE, I'VE ALWAYS BELIEVED IN THE CONCEPT OF A *FINITE* DEGREE OF MAGIC, AND HAVING EXPENDED MYSELF SO MUCH THESE PAST CENTURIES, I AM *REDUCED* TO, I'D SUPPOSE, LITTLE MORE THAN A COMMON *MAGE*.

ONE WOULD GUESS I'M STILL CAPABLE OF A FEW MINOR MIRACLES, BUT NOTHING ON ANY *COSMIC PLANE*.
I REALLY CAN'T SAY I AM *SORRY* ABOUT THAT. I NEVER *WANTED* MY POWERS, YOU KNOW. THEY CAME IN HANDY, NOW AND THEN, USEFUL QUITE OFTEN.
HOWEVER, I BELIEVE THAT I CAN GO THROUGH LIFE QUITE HAPPILY *WITHOUT* BEING ABLE TO PULL A HAT FULL OF RABBITS OUT OF THIN AIR.

SORCERY ISN'T *ALL* IT'S CRACKED UP TO BE, M'DEAR. TAKE IT FROM SOMEONE WHO--
AHHH, I SEE YOU HAVE *BETTER* THINGS ON YOUR MIND THAN A FOOLISH OLD MAN. GOOD FOR YOU, GIRL. *GOOD* FOR YOU!

YOU CAN'T IMAGINE THE PLEASURE I FEEL KNOWING YOU ARE HAPPY AT LONG LAST.
BUT NOW I THINK WE'D BEST RETURN MR. RUSSELL TO HIS HOME. I AM SORRY AN INNOCENT PERSON HAD TO BECOME INVOLVED IN ALL THIS, BUT IT WAS THE ONLY WAY I COULD PREVENT MORGAN FROM TOTALLY GETTING OUT OF HAND.

BESIDES, SHE WOULD HAVE FOUND MR. RUSSELL ON HER OWN, AND IT'S BEST THAT WE WERE ON HAND TO MAKE SURE HE SURVIVED HIS RATHER STRANGE ENCOUNTER.
HOWEVER, I ALSO THINK IT BEST THAT HE DOES NOT REMEMBER WHAT HAS HAPPENED. WE'LL ALL REST EASIER THAT WAY.
GOODBYE, LAD. PERHAPS WE'LL ALL MEET AGAIN ON A HAP-PIER NOTE.

AND NOW, M'DEAR, I DO THINK WE SHOULD RE-TURN HOME.
JESSICA? JESSICA!
AHHH, THE YOUNG...
IF ONLY I WAS THEIR AGE AGAIN.
NEXT ISSUE: WHO MURDERED JONATHAN DREW?

When young Jessica Drew was dying, her scientist-father injected her with a highly evolved serum of spider blood. The irradiated blood not only cured her, but changed her into the fearsome DARK ANGEL OF NIGHT.

Stan Lee PRESENTS: **THE MYSTERIOUS SPIDER-WOMAN!**

MARV WOLFMAN-WRITER/EDITOR • C. INFANTINO-ARTIST • LEIALOHA & GORDON-INKS • PARKO-LETTERS • G. WEIN-COLORS

july 4, 1978...

IT BEGINS JULY 2nd, 2:30 P.M.

IT IS A TYPICALLY HOT DAY IN LOS ANGELES. WEATHER FORECASTERS HAVE BEEN PREDICTING A RECORD-BREAKING 109 DEGREES. YET, INTO THIS EXCRUCIATING DRY HEAT, WE FIND JERRY HUNT, JESSICA DREW, AND THE MYSTERIOUS MAN CALLED MAGNUS...

MY LIFE IS CHANGING SO QUICKLY, I'VE HARDLY HAD TIME TO THINK...

WHAT'S THERE TO THINK ABOUT, DARLING? WE'VE SOMEHOW FOUND EACH OTHER...

...AND FOR SOME CRAZY REASON, WE SEEM TO BE IN LOVE.

WHAT ELSE IS THERE TO KNOW?

I WISH I KNEW... I REALLY WISH I KNEW.

PERHAPS UNTIL NOW, MY LIFE HAS BEEN SO INSANE THAT I CANNOT EASILY ACCEPT SANITY.
BUT I KNOW THAT WHEN I AM WITH YOU THAT EVERYTHING INSIDE ME IS PEACEFUL.

I NO LONGER FEEL LIKE A CAGED ANIMAL... ONE WHO ACTS ON THE WHIMS OF THE HIGH EVOLUTIONARY...OR HYDRA... OR ANY OF THE OTHERS WHO HAVE TRIED TO CONTROL MY LIFE.

PERHAPS, AT LONG LAST, MY PAST IS OVER AND DONE WITH-- PERHAPS NOW I CAN BE MYSELF... EXPLORE THIS NEW WORLD, AND LEARN WHO I REALLY AM.
YOU WON'T HAVE TO SEARCH ALONE. NOT ANY LONGER.

JESSICA, I'VE CONTACTED SHIELD-- THEY SAY THEY'RE WILLING TO GIVE US SOME PRECIOUS COMPUTER TIME.
I BELIEVE WE MAY BE ABLE TO BURY YOUR PAST-- FOREVER.
DO YOU MEAN--?
MR. HUNT, DO YOU THINK IT WISE?

HOW CAN YOU EVEN ASK THAT, MAGNUS? OF COURSE, IT'S IMPORTANT!
OUR COMPUTERS CAN SORT OUT ALL THE INFORMATION ABOUT JESSICA'S FATHER.

IT MAY FINALLY PINPOINT HIS MURDERER.
AND ONCE THAT IS DONE, ONCE JESSICA'S LAST TIE WITH THE PAST IS OVER...
...THEN THERE'S SOMETHING VERY IMPORTANT I WANT TO ASK HER.

JERRY HUNT, YOU ARE AN ADORABLE, CONSIDERATE MAN...
AND I LOVE YOU FOR THAT!

JULY 2ND. 4:08 P.M.
SHIELD LABS, SACRAMENTO...
THESE ARE THE MAXI-COMS, HON.
ONE BILLION DOLLARS WORTH OF CIRCUITS AND TUBES, ALL WORKING FOR YOU.
MR. HUNT, I'M AFRAID WE NO LONGER USE TUBES IN COMPUTERS...

STARK INTERNATIONAL DEVELOPED AN ENTIRELY NEW SYSTEM FOR-- AHHH, THE READ-OUT.
WE'LL ACTUALLY LEARN WHO KILLED MY FATHER?
NOT QUITE, JESSIE. WE FEED IN ALL THE KNOWN DATA.

MY WORD... HOW STRANGE. ALL THE TAB PRINTED OUT IS PYROTECHNICS.
WHAT ON EARTH DOES THAT MEAN?

JULY 2ND. 8:15 P.M.
THE CONFERENCE ROOM AT PYROTECHNICS, INC.
DAMN IT, MAN. WE'RE SO CLOSE TO SUCCESS, AND NOW WE'VE GOT THIS SPIDER-WOMAN CREATURE BREATHING DOWN OUR NECKS.
SHE'S ATTACKED ME-- TWICE. SHE'S BEEN SEEN PROWLING ABOUT HERE-- SHE WAS EVEN RESPONSIBLE FOR THE BLOW-OUT IN SECTION 4.
ON TOP OF ALL THAT, SHE'S CONNECTED US WITH JONATHAN DREW'S DEATH. I TELL YOU, HE'S A WORSE PAIN DEAD THAN HE WAS ALIVE.

STOP RANTING, WYATT. WE NEEDED DREW... NEEDED THE KNOWLEDGE HE HAD.

I AGREE WITH BILLINGSLEY, CONGRESSMAN. BESIDES, NOTHING CAN PREVENT OUR OPERATION FROM BEING A SUCCESS.

GENERAL GASPAR, I SINCERELY HOPE NOT.
BUT I WOULD REST EASIER IF THAT CREATURE WERE GOTTEN RID OF.
THERE IS SOMETHING ABOUT HER THAT... BOTHERS ME... AND I'LL BE DAMNED IF I KNOW WHAT IT IS.

ALL RIGHT, GENTLEMEN, I'VE STILL GOT THE CAMP TO INSPECT. LET US CALL IT A NIGHT, SHALL WE?
SO, WYATT IS BEHIND MY FATHER'S DEATH. I THOUGHT SO ALL ALONG!

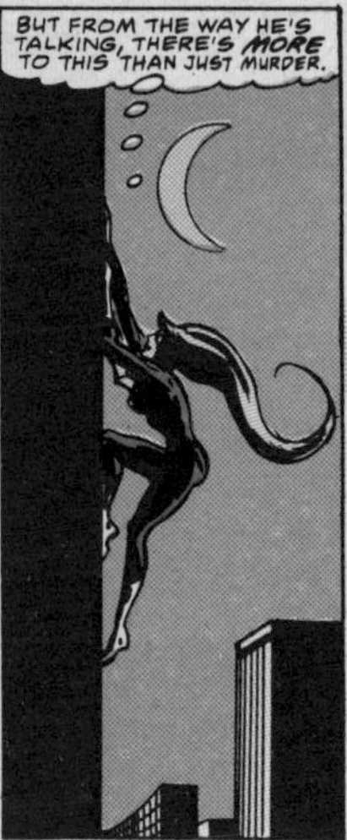
BUT FROM THE WAY HE'S TALKING, THERE'S MORE TO THIS THAN JUST MURDER.

I THINK I'LL FOLLOW THE CONGRESSMAN AND SEE WHAT THAT SLIMY SCHEMER IS INVOLVED WITH NOW.

PERFECT! JESSIE'S LATCHED ONTO HER TARGET... NOW TO CHECK OUT MINE!
GOOD LUCK, DARLING.

JULY 3RD. 12:21 A.M.
BARBED WIRE FENCE... AND GUARDS... BUT THEY AREN'T DRESSED IN ANY U.S. MILITARY GARB.
WHAT IS ALL THIS ABOUT?

GENERAL DANVERS, HOW IS IT GOING?
ALL RECRUITS ARE READY, CONGRESSMAN. READY AND ANXIOUS!
WELL, TOMORROW IS THE DAY, GENERAL. THEY WON'T BE ANXIOUS FOR TOO MUCH LONGER.

CONGRESSMAN, WHEN WILL THE INJECTIONS BE READY?
TOMORROW, BEFORE WE STRIKE.

INJECTIONS? THIS DOESN'T MAKE ANY SENSE.
BUT I DON'T DARE STAY HERE MUCH LONGER... AT ANY MOMENT, I MAY BE SPOTTED.
I'VE GOT TO TELL JERRY WHAT I'VE LEARNED...

JULY 2ND. 10:15 P.M.
JESSIE SHOULD HAVE HER HANDS FILLED FOLLOWING WYATT...
...WHILE I MAKE IT TO PYRO'S RECORDS ROOM.
AHH, THE PERFECT PLAN APPROACHES.

THERE IS A MOMENTARY STRUGGLE, AND THEN...
NOT BAD, THE SIZE IS ALMOST PERFECT.
AS LONG AS I DON'T HAVE TO RUN TOO FAST, THAT IS.
BOUND INSIDE A STORAGE CLOSET, THE STILL-SURPRISED GUARD FINDS HIMSELF VIRTUALLY NAKED, AND HE WONDERS HOW HE IS GOING TO EXPLAIN ALL THIS TO HIS SUPERIORS.

THE OTHERS FROM THE CONFERENCE ROOM ARE FINALLY LEAVING.
HOPEFULLY, NO ONE WILL SPOT ME AS A RINGER.
WELL, GENERAL GASPAR, THE FOURTH IS ONLY A COUPLE DAYS AWAY.
MY MEN ARE PREPARED TO GIVE A PYROTECHNICAL DISPLAY THAT NO ONE CAN EXPECT. DON'T YOU WORRY, MR. BILLINGSLEY.

NOW, WHAT'S THAT SUPPOSED TO MEAN?
SOMETHING TELLS ME THAT THIS PLACE ISN'T JUST INVOLVED WITH JONATHAN DREW'S MURDER.

SOMETHING'S BREWING HERE... BUT I SUPPOSE I'LL JUST HAVE TO WAIT TO LEARN WHAT THAT IS.
SURE HOPE JESSIE'S ALL RIGHT. I WORRY ABOUT HER. HER POWERS MAY BE BEYOND IMAGINATION, BUT SHE KNOWS SO VERY LITTLE ABOUT THE WAYS OF OUR CIVILIZATION.

AND FROM WHAT SHE'S TOLD ME OF WUNDAGORE-- OUR WAYS MAY BE A HELLUVA LOT MORE DANGEROUS.
HMMM... THINK I'VE GOTTEN JUST ABOUT EVERYTHING NOW.

NO ONE OUT HERE, AND THAT MEANS THEY HAVEN'T YET FOUND THE POOR GUARD I WAYLAID.
WITH LUCK, I SHOULD BE OUT OF HERE LONG BEFORE THEY DO.

JULY 3RD. 4:18 A.M.
THESE PHOTOGRAPHS ARE QUITE INFORM-ATIVE, MR. HUNT.
ESPECIALLY THIS ONE, JERRY.
I THOUGHT YOU'D WANT TO SEE IT, HONEY.

IT CONCLUSIVELY PROVES THAT CONGRESS-MAN WYATT KNEW YOUR FATHER...
...DESPITE EVERY LIE HE'S TOLD YOU TO DATE.

BUT WHAT WORRIES ME, JERRY...
...IS WHAT MY FATHER DID FOR WYATT.

YEAH, THAT'S BEEN PUZZLING ME, TOO. LOOK, WE KNOW THEY'VE SOME-THING PLANNED FOR JULY 4TH. BUT WHAT?
A ROBBERY? A MILITARY-PRECISION THEFT?

WHAT DO YOU THINK, MAGNUS?
I BELIEVE THERE ARE THINGS BETTER NOT REVEALED.

THAT DOES IT, MAGNUS! IT SEEMS TO ME THAT YOU'VE KNOWN JUST ABOUT EVERY-THING... BUT YOU'VE NEVER TOLD US A THING!
BECAUSE OF YOU, I'VE FALLEN INTO TRAPS, I'VE BEEN ABUSED, ALMOST KILLED, AND TOTALLY CONFUSED.

AND I STILL DON'T KNOW ABOUT YOU AND MORGAN LE FAY! DURING OUR FIGHT SHE CALLED YOU HER TEACHER.
THAT WOULD MAKE YOU-- MERLIN THE MAGICIAN!
MERLIN? JESSICA, MY DEAR, THE OLD MAGE WOULD HAVE LOVED THAT.

NO, MY DEAR, I'M NOT MERLIN, AND YOU MISUNDERSTOOD MORGAN.
YOU SEE, I WAS NOT HER TEACHER-- BUT HER STUDENT!
SHE TAUGHT ME THE DARK ARTS... AND WHEN I REALIZED THEY WERE EVIL, I FLED FROM HER SIGHT, TAKING THE BOOK OF DARK-HOLD WITH ME.
BUT, YOU MAY BE RIGHT, I HAVE BEEN SECRETIVE... FOR A REASON.
YOU WERE DYING OF RADIATION POISONING, AND YOUR POOR FATHER VALIANTLY SOUGHT A CURE.
...UNTIL THE MAN WHO WOULD SOME-DAY BECOME THE HIGH EVOLUTIONARY CONVINCED YOUR FATHER HE NEEDED A REST.
JONATHAN, YOU'RE NOT HELPING JESSICA. GO AWAY... REST... I'LL WATCH HER, BELIEVE ME.
BESIDES, I HAVE A FEW IDEAS THAT MAY SAVE JESSICA... AND I COULD USE THE TIME ALONE TO WORK THEM OUT.
...ALL RIGHT, MY FRIEND. I... I TRUST YOU.
JONATHAN DREW VANISHED AFTER THAT. HIS PATH SOMEHOW LED HIM TO WORK IN THE BRITISH MUSEUM, AND THROUGH THEM, PYRO-TECHNICS.
IT SEEMS ONE OF HIS DISCOVERIES WAS CONNECTED WITH SOMETHING PYRO-TECHNICS WAS WORKING ON.
AND THAT, MY DEAR, IS ALL I KNOW ABOUT YOUR FATHER.

BUT THAT WAS YEARS AGO WHEN I WAS A CHILD. WHAT HAPPENED TO HIM AFTER THAT?
OBVIOUSLY, HE MUST HAVE BEEN KEPT CAPTIVE AT PYROTECHNICS, WORKING FOR THEM AGAINST HIS OWN WILL.
PERHAPS HE TRIED TO ESCAPE... AND THAT IS WHEN THEY KILLED HIM.

THAT DOESN'T SEEM TO MAKE SENSE, MAGNUS. WHY WOULD THEY KILL IF--
JERRY! SHUT UP.
WHAT?

I--I'M SORRY, I WAS TRYING TO THINK... THERE'S SOMETHING I ALMOST REMEMB-- WAIT!
I'VE GOT IT!

WITHOUT A PAUSE, JESSICA DREW OPENS THE WINDOW AND LEAPS SKYWARD, HER LITHE FORM GLIDES ON THE EARLY MORNING BREEZE.
JESSICA! COME BACK! WHERE ARE YOU GOING?
HER EYES NARROW IN DETERMINATION. SHE HAS A MISSION, AND IT IS ONE THAT MUST BE SOLVED BEFORE THE NIGHT IS DONE.

MR. HUNT...JERRY, LET HER GO.
WHATEVER IT IS SHE HAS TO DO-- SHE'D BEST DO IT ALONE.
BUT--?
YOU DO NOT UNDERSTAND. I BELIEVE JESSICA DREW IS ABOUT TO MEET HER DESTINY-- FACE-TO-FACE!

A DESTINY THAT BEGINS WITHIN THE ESTATE BELONGING TO CONGRESSMAN JAMES T. WYATT...
IT IS ALL OVER, WYATT. I KNOW EVERYTHING!
YOU! YOU'RE STILL HOUNDING ME!
BASH!
NO MORE, CONGRESSMAN. I'M HERE TO PUNISH YOU--
FOR YOUR JULY FOURTH PLANS...
OH, GOD-- YOU KNOW ABOUT THEM?

I KNOW MUCH MORE, CONGRESSMAN. I KNOW YOU MURDERED MY FATHER!
Y-YOUR FATHER! JONATHAN DREW WAS YOUR FATHER? OH DEAR LORD... DEAR, SWEET LORD...

NOW, TELL ME EVERYTHING!
I-I CAN'T... THEY'LL KILL ME!

YOU WILL TALK... YOU WILL REVEAL EVERYTHING!
PLEASE DON'T MAKE ME SAY ANYTHING... DON'T... MAKE ME... UNGGHHHH...

JULY 3RD. 10:38 A.M.
BUT, YOU'VE FAILED--
AND FAILED MISERABLY!
THE SPIDER-WOMAN!
SOMEONE-- STOP HER!
THE BOARD ROOM AT PYROTECHNICS, INC.
YOU THOUGHT YOU COULD ACTUALLY GET AWAY WITH YOUR MAD SCHEME, DIDN'T YOU?

NEEDN'T WORRY, GENERAL--
I ALWAYS CARRY A RATHER DEADLY LITTLE TOY WITH ME...
THE SAME CALIBER MY COMPANY DESIGNED FOR YOUR MEN.

YOUR WEAPON IS USELESS... IF YOU CAN'T USE IT.!
WHAT?
ZDAK

SHUT UP AND LISTEN, ALL OF YOU! MY VENOM BLAST CAN EITHER STUN OR KILL.
IF ONE OF YOU MISERABLE SPECIMENS OF HUMANKIND EVEN RAISES A FINGER, I PROMISE MY NEXT BLAST WILL NOT BE TO STUN.

I SUGGEST YOU SIT DOWN AND BEGIN TALKING. I WANT TO KNOW EVERYTHING ABOUT TOMORROW'S ACTION!
BUT YOU'LL HEAR NOTHING, FRILL.

TH-THAT VOICE?
WHAT? GAS!?!
IT'S NUMBING ME... CAN'T STAND... STAND...

GOOD WORK, BROTHER GRIMM.
STOW THE COMPLIMENTS, BLUE-EYES.
JUST HAND OVER THE GREEN-BACKS, AND LEMME BE ON MY WAY WITH A "HARDY HI YO," WELL, YOU KNOW THE REST.

JULY 3RD. 10:46 P.M.
A CONVOY OF UNMARKED TRUCKS ROLL OVER A GRAVEL ROAD TOWARD A SECRET MILITARY BASE SOMEWHERE OUTSIDE LOS ANGELES, CALIFORNIA.

ABOARD THE CANVAS-BACKED VEHICLES, SIT A COMPLEMENT OF SOLDIERS WHOSE UNIFORMS REVEAL NOTHING OF THEIR BASE OF ORIGIN.

AHHH, I SEE YOU'RE AWAKE, SPIDER-WOMAN. GOOD, YOU'RE IN TIME TO WITNESS THE MOST IMPORTANT JULY 4TH IN 202 YEARS.
WYATT?
CONGRESSMAN WYATT, SPIDER-WOMAN. PLEASE, THE TITLE IS VERY IMPORTANT.
OH YES, I SUGGEST THE NEXT TIME YOU LEAVE A PRISONER BEHIND, TIE THEM UP, DON'T MERELY LOCK THEM IN A ROOM.
THERE WAS A TELEPHONE QUITE HANDY FOR ME TO CALL MY ASSOCIATES.

WHAT IS THIS ALL ABOUT?
NO HARM IN TELLING YOU, SEEING THAT YOU WILL SOON BE DEAD... BESIDES, YOUR FATHER IS RESPONSIBLE FOR TODAY'S HAPPENING.
WHAT?
THAT IS CORRECT. HE HAPPENED TO MENTION HIS SPIDER-EXTRACT SERUM WHEN HE WENT TO WORK IN THE MUSEUM.

WE REASONED, IF HE COULD POSSIBLY CREATE AN ANTIDOTE FOR RADIATION POISONING -- WE COULD USE IT...
...FOR OUR PURPOSES, OF COURSE.
WE TOOK YOUR POOR FATHER AWAY, KEPT HIM DRUGGED UNTIL HE PERFECTED THE SERUM. AND, WOULD YOU BELIEVE, HE NEVER ONCE REALIZED OUR TRUE INTENT?
YOUR FATHER WAS A NAIVE FOOL!

YOU SEE, WE HAD PERFECTED A WORKING NEUTRON DEVICE AND HE CREATED THE METHOD OUR SOLDIERS WOULD USE TO SURVIVE ITS DEADLY RADIATION.
WYATT, LOOK!
WHAT IS IT, MAN?
THE TRUCKS ARE RETURNING!

BUT THE MEN WERE HEADING TO PYRO-TECHNICS FOR THEIR INJECTIONS.

DAMN! THE DOOR IS TOO THICK! I CAN'T BREAK THROUGH IT.
WHAM

THOSE SOLDIERS-- THEY'RE NOT OUR MEN!
WHO ARE THEY?
IT DOESN'T MAKE ANY DIFFERENCE!

THIS IS WYATT! WE'VE BEEN INVADED!

ALL PERSONNEL-- INTO THE COMPOUND! FULL ATTACK!
ALL RIGHT, GUYS--YOU HEARD THE MAN. THAT GIVES US ONLY MINUTES TO DEMOLISH THIS BASE.
C'MON! MOVE!
JERRY HUNT'S ORDERS RING THROUGH THE COURTYARD...

AND, A MOMENT LATER...
ALL RIGHT, WYATT. FREE SPIDER-WOMAN--NOW!
WHO ARE YOU?
NEVER MIND THAT! DO AS I SAY!

I'LL DO THAT-- AND MORE, YOU FOOL!

JERRY, STOP HIM! IF HE PRESSES THAT BUTTON, HE'LL HAVE DOOMED US BOTH!

STAND BACK, BEAUTIFUL! I DON'T WANT TO ACCIDENTAL-LY HIT YOU!
UNGGHHH!
YOU'RE TOO LATE! I'M TAKING ALL OF YOU WITH ME!
BUDDA! BUDDA!
BAM! BAM!

BUT WHY-- WHY ARE YOU DOING THIS? YOU WERE A RESPECTED CONGRESSMAN...
UHHHH... RESPECT? THAT DOESN'T MEAN A DAMN THING-- I WANTED MONEY! POWER! I WANTED IT ALL... AND--GASP--AND IT WAS ALMOST MINE. I WAS ALMOST ABLE TO TOUCH IT!

ARE YOU---INSANE?
...INSANE...UHHH...NO, THE DREAM WASN'T...INSANE. IT--CHOKE--COULD HAVE WORKED.
GASP WE COULD HAVE OVERRUN EVERY MAJOR MILITARY BASE AT THE STROKE OF--UHHHHH--MIDNIGHT.
AMERICA WOULD HAVE--UHHH...FALLEN...AND I--GASP--I WOULD HAVE HAD EVERYTHING I...EVER...WANTED.
JERRY--LET ME ASK HIM--WHAT ABOUT MY FATHER? WHO KILLED HIM?

WHAT--UHHH--DIFFERENCE COULD IT MAKE?
FOR GOD'S SAKE, WYATT--ANSWER!
I...I KILLED HIM...HE TRIED TO ESCAPE...UHHH...BEFORE THE FINAL TESTING WAS DONE. I HAD...HAD NO CHOICE...

...NO CHOICE...NO...UHHHHHHH...
HE'S DEAD!
AND WE'D BETTER GET OUT OF HERE FAST.

"THAT WAS THE DESTRUCT BUTTON HE PRESSED. WHO KNOWS HOW MUCH TIME WE HAVE!"
THE TWO RACE FROM THE BUILDING, SPIDER-WOMAN THROUGH THE COOL MIST OF NIGHT, JERRY HUNT SHOUTING TO HIS MEN TO BOARD THE TRUCKS THAT HAD BROUGHT THEM HERE...
...WITHIN SECONDS, THEY ARE GONE.

AND JUST BARELY IN TIME...
JULY 4TH. 12:01 A.M.

JULY 4TH. 10:00 A.M.
SHIELD HEADQUARTERS.
...OUR MEN ARRIVED JUST IN TIME TO STOP THEIR SOLDIERS ON THE WAY TO PYROTECHNICS, THEN WE TOOK THEIR PLACES. THAT'S ABOUT IT!
DID WE ROUND-UP THE OTHERS, COLONEL?
IF YA MEAN THE CREEPS ON THAT LIST YA PHOTOGRAPHED-- YEAH! AND WE GOT SOME NICE SIGNED CONFESSIONS.
YOU DID A GOOD JOB, HUNT... YA MIGHT EVEN GET A GOLD STAR FOR THIS ONE.

AS FOR YOU, LITTLE LADY-- I HEARD ABOUT YOUR FATHER-- BUT MEBBE YA MADE UP FOR HIS DEATH A BIT BY FINDIN' HIS MURDERERS.

COLONEL FURY, I FOUND MY FATHER'S KILLER, WHICH ALLOWS HIM TO REST IN PEACE...

...BUT I CAN NOW LIVE IN PEACE-- BECAUSE I FOUND THE MAN I LOVE!
NEXT ISSUE
A BOLD NEW DIRECTION FOR MARVEL'S DARK ANGEL...
THE MAN WHO COULD NOT DIE!

When young Jessica Drew was dying, her scientist-father injected her with a highly evolved serum of spider blood. The irradiated blood not only cured her, but changed her into the fearsome DARK ANGEL OF NIGHT.

Stan Lee PRESENTS: THE MYSTERIOUS SPIDER-WOMAN!

MARY WOLFMAN / WRITER/EDITOR | CARMINE INFANTINO / PENCILS | AL GORDON / INKS | COSTANZA, LETTERER / F. MOULY, COLORIST | JIM SHOOTER / CONSULTING ED.

PLEASE, DON'T MAKE ME SHOOT YOU HERE... IT WOULD ALL BE SO-- SO WASTED.
DON'T LOOK AT ME LIKE THAT, LORD, I TOLD YOU I HAVEN'T ANY CHOICE... I HAVE TO KILL...

YOU WON'T MAKE THIS EASY FOR ME, WILL YOU? LOOK, WHAT IF I PROMISE NOT TO CHAIN YOU?

WILL YOU COME WITH ME?
I-I'LL EXPLAIN AGAIN WHY YOU HAVE TO DIE...
WHY I HAVE TO DIE AS WELL.
"I EXPLAINED, DIDN'T I, THAT FOR ME, AT LEAST, IT BEGAN ON A DAY AS HOT AS TODAY IS COLD. HOT WITH THE MUGGY SWEAT OF BATTLE...

"...HOT WITH THE BLAZING FIRE POWER OF GUNS.
"I'LL NEVER FORGET THE DAY-- AUGUST 12, 1778. TWO HUNDRED YEARS AGO--TODAY!.
"I--I WAS SENT TO SPY ON THE BRITISH, AND, LORD-- WHAT I SAW STILL HAUNTS ME NOW. THE BRITISH WERE WAITING FOR MY BRIGADE ATOP FOWLER'S HILL...

"MY MEN WERE MARCHING RIGHT TOWARD THEIR DEATHS. I COULD HAVE WARNED THEM IN TIME...

"BUT THAT WAS WHEN I REALIZED IF I DID, THE REDCOATS WOULD OPEN FIRE ON ME!

"SO I REMAINED SILENT AND WATCHED MY FRIENDS, MY NEIGHBORS-- I WATCHED THEM FALL FROM A DISTANCE AS THEIR LIVES WERE CUT SHORT.

"I SAID NOTHING, BUT IT DID NOT TAKE LONG FOR THE PEOPLE TO GUESS WHAT HAD HAPPENED...

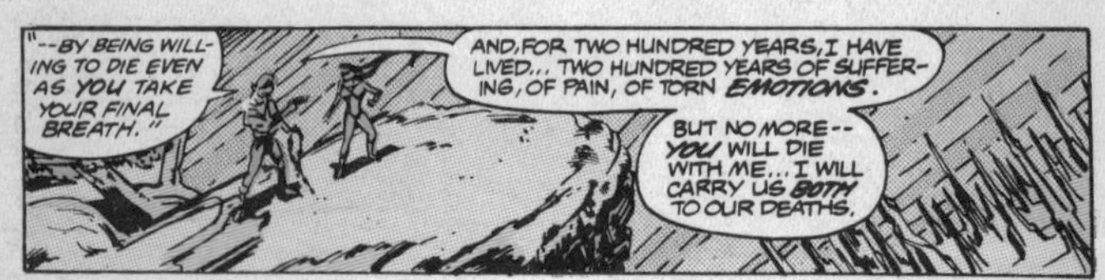

I'VE TRIED KILLING MYSELF MORE TIMES THAN I CAN REMEMBER--I'VE BECOME A MASTER OF INGENUITY--
--BUT, EACH ATTEMPT FAILED... AND FRUSTRATES... AND GOADS ME ON MORE AND MORE.
HOW MANY MORE ATTEMPTS MUST I MAKE? I DO NOT KNOW...; BUT I CAN SEE NO WAY OUT--UNLESS I KEEP TRYING.
SO STRANGE--HE WANTS TO END HIS LIFE EVEN AS MY LIFE BEGINS.

FOR PERHAPS THE FIRST TIME IN ALL MY YEARS I AM MYSELF--WITHOUT ANOTHER ORDERING ME... PROTECTING ME--GUIDING ME.
TO THINK... TO THINK--
"SEVERAL HOURS AGO, DEATH WAS THE FURTHEST THOUGHT I COULD HAVE..."
I DON'T KNOW WHEN I HAVE ENJOYED MYSELF MORE. THANK YOU FOR BRINGING ME HERE, JERRY.
HECK, JESSIE, I'M GETTING AS MUCH A KICK OUT OF THIS AS YOU ARE.

Y'KNOW SOMETHING, I'D ENJOY ANYTHING JUST BEING WITH YOU.
YOU'RE UNLIKE OTHER WOMEN... YOU MAY BE INSECURE ABOUT SOME THINGS... AND BELIEVE ME THOSE INSECURITIES WILL VANISH AFTER AWHILE...
...BUT YOU'RE IN COMMAND OF YOURSELF--YOU'RE YOUR OWN PERSON.
I COULDN'T STAND A WOMAN WHO WASN'T INDEPENDENT HERSELF--AND STILL LOVING... GIVING...
I HATE TO USE THE HOLLYWOOD CATCH-PHRASES, THEY'RE SO TRITE THEY'RE RIDICULOUS--
BUT WE BOTH RESPECT EACH OTHER... CARE FOR EACH OTHER--WE EACH HAVE OUR OWN SPACE, AND--
JERRY, DO YOU HEAR SOMETHING? A CRY--?

JESSICA--LOOK! SOME NUT'S TRYING TO PROVE SOMETHING--STANDING ON THE CABLE CAR--!
WHAT SHOULD WE DO?
DO? YOU'RE THE ONLY ONE WHO CAN RESCUE HIM-- THE ONLY ONE WHO CAN HELP.
"I DUCKED INTO A CORNER AND CHANGED INTO THAT COSTUME--THAT DISGUISE THAT MAKES ME THE SPIDER-WOMAN.

"HER POWERS WERE NEEDED NOW--
"--FOR ONLY SHE COULD RESCUE THAT MAN...

NO, DON'T! I WANT TO DIE! LET ME FALL!

DIDN'T YOU HEAR ME? I WANT TO DIE!

NO ONE CAN STOP ME--
--SO WHY TRY?
WAIT!

"I CAN'T REMEMBER HOW LONG I WAS UNCONSCIOUS... BUT I REMEMBER AS I SLOWLY AWOKE, MY BONES WEAK WITH PAIN...

"... HE WAS STANDING THERE IN THE FIRE--UNSCATHED--BUT WAS HE LAUGHING IN MAD VICTORY OVER DEATH--

"--OR CRYING?"

BEHIND THEM IS A SUDDEN GROWL. THEY SPIN, AND SEE--

STAND BACK, BRUIN--
THERE WILL BE NO MORE
FIGHTING TODAY!

DIDN'T YOU
HEAR ME,
BEAST?
IT STILL CLAWS
THE AIR--IT
WON'T SETTLE
FOR A
STALEMATE.
THEN I
HAVE NO
CHOICE!

I CAN
ONLY HOPE
MY VENOM
BLAST
STUNS THE
POOR BEAST
AND DOESN'T
SLAY HIM--
HE FIGHTS
NOT FOR
VENGEANCE
... BUT OUT OF
FEAR THAT
WE'VE COME
TO HARM HIM.

YOU FOUGHT
FOR ME...
WHY?
I--I WANTED
TO KILL--
WHEN THE
BEAR FIRST
APPEARED--
YOU ATTACKED
IT--
--THOUGH YOU KNEW
YOU WOULD NOT DIE.
YOU TRIED TO
SAVE ME,
SAMUEL DAVIS.
COULD I DO
ANY LESS?

ACCORDING TO YOUR CURSE-- YOU MUST FIND SOMEONE WILLING TO DIE WITH YOU.
I AM WILLING.
BUT--?
ASK NO FURTHER QUESTIONS-- YOU ATTEMPTED TO SAVE MY LIFE--
YOU HAVE PROVEN THAT YOU CAN CARE.
YOU HAVE DEMONSTRATED THAT YOU ARE NOT A COWARD!

ARE YOU CERTAIN? I--I CAN'T LET YOU--
IT IS NO LONGER YOUR DECISION. JUMP!
THEY FALL AND THE GROUND RUSHES UP TO MEET THESE TWO.

BUT THERE IS THE SOUND OF CHAIN SNAPPING... THE MOVEMENT OF ONE BODY STRETCHING OUT TO MEET THE COLD, CRISP AIR OF NIGHT--
--AND THE GENTLE, SILENT SOUND OF ONE FORM SLIDING FREE WHILE ANOTHER FALLS TOWARD HIS SPECIAL KIND OF FREEDOM.

HE HAS PROVEN HIMSELF... PROVEN HE IS NO COWARD... PROVEN HE COULD CARE... AND IN CARING, HE FOUND A WOMAN WHO COULD CARE IN TURN--
AND THAT CARING WAS ALL THAT WAS NECESSARY FOR ONE CURSE TO END...
...AND FOR AN ETERNITY OF PEACEFUL SLEEP TO BEGIN...
FIN.

MARV WOLFMAN, WRITER/EDITOR . CARMINE INFANTINO, PENCILS . AL GORDON, INKS . JOHN COSTANZA, letters . GEORGE ROUSSOS, colors

GUNTHER MALONE IS A MASS OF TINGLING NERVES THAT MOVE HIM EVER ON. HE HAS TO RUN... TO HIDE, BUT THE TRUTH OF THE MATTER SIMPLY IS, THERE IS NO PLACE HE CAN HIDE. GUNTHER MALONE IS CAUGHT IN A MAZE OF LIES AND DECEITS THAT OFFER ONLY ONE POSSIBLE EXIT-- DEATH!

BUT, IT IS ALREADY TOO LATE AS GUNTHER MALONE MOMENTARILY DISCOVERS WHEN HE STEPS FROM THE ALLEY'S DARK SHADOWS--

--INTO A PATH OF BLAZING LEAD!

THE SUIT!

GOT THE, STINKIN' DOUBLE-CROSSER!

COULDN'T MISS HITTING THAT SUIT OF HIS-- EVEN WITH MY EYES CLOSED.

MARCUS EVANIER POURS THROUGH THE PAPER AS HE HAS DONE EVERY DAY FOR THE PAST SIX MONTHS... LOOKING, SEARCHING, HOPING TO FIND--
A JOB! LINDA, LOOK--
"SALESMAN WANTED FOR IMMEDIATE SUCCESS."
DO YOU THINK I SHOULD TRY?
GANGSTER GUNTHER MALONE SLAIN!
TRY? MARCUS, WHO WAS THE BEST SALESMAN AT "SADETSKY NYLONS" FOR THIRTY YEARS BEFORE THEY FOLDED? ONLY MARCUS EVANIER.

BUT--
NO "BUTS," MARCUS. THIS IS A SIGN! GO...TRY!
YOU DON'T UNDERSTAND, LINDA. A SALESMAN CAN'T LOOK LIKE I DO NOW. I DON'T EVEN HAVE A SUIT.

I WOULD BE LAUGHED OUT OF THE STORE.
I CAN'T GO LOOKING LIKE THIS--I CAN'T...
SO, WE GET YOU A SUIT.

HOW? WE CAN'T AFFORD TO RENT ONE.
YOU THINK MY BROTHER WILL CHARGE YOU?

LINDA--? HEY, LONG TIME. HOW'S IT GOIN'? OH, I SEE... I DIDN'T KNOW IT WAS THAT BAD. YOU SHOULD HAVE TOLD--
HUH? A SUIT? LAST TIME I HAD A SUIT I WAS--
HEY, SIS, WAIT A BIT. MAYBE I CAN BORROW ONE FOR YOU... ONLY NEED IT A DAY?
P.D.

YEAH, I'M SURE I CAN GET IT FOR YOU.
HEY, WHAT'S A BROTHER FOR, EH?

GUNTHER MALONE IS WHEELED INTO THE POLICE AUTOPSY ROOM, HIS BODY COLD AS HIS HEART WHEN HE WAS ALIVE.
THREE BULLETS THROUGH THE LEFT VENTRICLE. HE WENT FAST.
ALL RIGHT, SEW HIM UP AND MOVE HIM ON TO THE MORGUE.
THINK IT'LL BE AN IMPROVE-MENT?
I DOUBT IT, BUT MAYBE SOMEONE'LL CLAIM HIM.

OUTSIDE, THE NIGHT IS WARM, A FULL MOON REFLECTS OFF THE DULL GREY STONE OF POLICE HEADQUARTERS...
...AND HIGHLIGHTS A SLIM FIGURE THAT GLIDES GRACEFULLY TOWARD THE IMPOSING EDIFICE, AND ALIGHTS WITHOUT THE SLIGHTEST SOUND.

THE WOMAN LISTENS AS THE DOCTORS CONCLUDE THEIR AUTOPSY...
THEN, HAVING LEARNED NOTHING, TAKES OFF INTO THE THICKENING BLACK OF NIGHT.

MARCUS, YOU'RE LOOKING GOOD.
THANKS, BILL. I'LL FEEL BETTER IF I GET THAT JOB TOMORROW.
I'VE GOT AN APPOINT-MENT.
YEAH, LINDA TOLD ME.

HEY, HERE'S THE SUIT... I THINK IT'LL FIT YOU, TOO.
YOU'LL RETURN IT TOMORROW? THEY'LL NEED IT BY THEN.
BILL, I--I DON'T KNOW HOW TO THANK YOU... I JUST MAY GET THAT JOB YET.

JUST COVER THOSE BULLET HOLES IN BACK AND YOU'LL DO FINE.
LISTEN, GOOD LUCK.
TH-THANKS... I'LL NEED IT.
PD

WEARING THIS SUIT MAKES ME FEEL LIKE A WINNER!
SOME-HOW I KNOW I'LL GET THAT JOB.
YESSIR-- FROM NOW ON, NOTHING IS GOING TO PUT DOWN MARCUS EVANIER-- NOTHING!

JAKE-- JAKE, TELL ME I'M GOIN' LOONEY. TELL ME ANYTHING BUT WHAT I'M LOOKIN' AT IS REAL--!
LOOK--IT'S IMPOSSIBLE... BUT THERE'S GUNTHER.
YOU CRAZY, ZIGGY? TH-THA-- SAME!
THAT SUIT! IT'S GOTTA BE GUNTHER...

HE HAD THAT SUIT MADE FOR HIM--ONLY ONE OF ITS KIND.
BUT WE KILLED HIM YESTERDAY. AT LEAST I THOUGHT WE DID.
WE DID! WE DID!
BUT LET'S KILL HIM AGAIN-- JUST TO MAKE SURE!

MARCUS EVANIER IS A HAPPY MAN AS HE MEETS HOWARD ASHLEY OF "ASHLEY BOOK DISTRIBUTORS."
YOU'RE THE KIND OF SALESMAN I'M LOOKING FOR, MARCUS-- NOT ONE OF THESE YOUNG KIDS WHO COULDN'T SELL A HOT WATER BAG TO AN ESKIMO.
YOU'RE HIRED!
I AM? I AM!! THANK YOU, MR. ASHLEY... THANK YOU!

JUST DO ME PROUD, MARCUS. HERE'S THE BOOK WE'RE PROMOTING THIS MONTH--
READ IT, ENJOY IT, AND SEE ME TO-MORROW.
LUCK: HOW TO FIND AND KEEP IT!

"LUCK: HOW TO FIND AND KEEP IT."
FIND AND KEEP IT!
MR. ASHLEY, SOMETHING TELLS ME THIS BOOK WILL BE VERY LUCKY FOR US BOTH.

IT'S BEEN SUCH A LONG TIME I THOUGHT I WAS GOING TO BE NERVOUS.
BUT, ONCE A SALESMAN-- ALWAYS A SALESMAN.
OOO.
I'VE GOT A JOB, MY CONFIDENCE IS RETURNING-- YESSIR, THINGS ARE LOOKING UP NOW.
HMMM, BETTER GET A GIFT FOR LINDA-- WITHOUT HER I'D NEVER HAVE SUCCEEDED.

LOOK, DON'T BELIEVE ME, BUT WE BOTH SAW 'IM.
GUNTHER'S ALIVE!
ALIVE! YOU STUPID, INSIGNIFICANT PUNKS!
I SEND YOU OUT TO KILL ONE MAN-- AND HE STILL LIVES?!?
GET OUT! GET OUT! KILL HIM AGAIN!
AND WHILE YOU'RE AT IT-- FIND THE MONEY HE STOLE FROM US!
Y-YES, BOSS.

BEHIND "LACY'S BAR AND GRILL" ON 4TH STREET AND ALVARADO IS A SMALL APARTMENT OWNED BY ONE "BENNY THE GIMP." BENNY IS A KNOWN PIGEON...
WHAT DO YOU KNOW OF GUNTHER MALONE? SPEAK! NOW!
CRIPES! IT'S A BROAD!
A BROAD CAN'T SMASH THROUGH WALLS, CAN SHE?
SHE IS, YOU STUPID DOLT.
WHO'RE YOU CALLING STUPID, STUPID?
I SAID I WANTED INFORMATION. WHAT HAPPENED TO THE MONEY GUNTHER MALONE STOLE? WHERE IS IT?
H-HEY, DON'T HURT US, LADY!
GUNTHER, HE BELONGED TO TOUGH LOOEY'S MOB... WE DON'T KNOW NOTHIN' ABOUT THEM.
REALLY!

AS MARCUS PROUDLY STRIDES HOME, HE NOTICES SOMETHING... STRANGE. HIS STEP QUICKENS... THE BLOOD IN HIS VEINS IS RUSHING -- HIS HEART IS WILDLY PUMPING...
HIS LEGS MAKE HIM TURN A CORNER WHICH HE DOESN'T WANT TO TURN...
ASTONISHED, HE REACHES OUT--TRIES TO STOP HIMSELF... BUT SOMEHOW, SOMEHOW, HE IS UNABLE.
HE CAN'T HELP HIMSELF! HE IS MOVING AGAINST HIS OWN WILL!

PASSERSBY OBSERVE HIS PREDICAMENT AND CONTINUE ON-- WHY GET INVOLVED WITH ANOTHER WEIRDO IN A CITY OF WEIRDOS!
MARCUS CALLS OUT--"PLEASE, SOMEONE--HELP ME!" THERE IS NO ANSWER AS HE BEGINS RUNNING DOWN 9TH STREET TOWARD THE EXCAVATION SITE...
SWEAT BEADS OFF MARCUS'S FRIGHTENED FACE--"LORD, WHAT IS HAPPENING TO ME?" HE CRIES. "WHAT IS HAPPENING TO ME?"

NEEDLESS TO SAY, THERE ISN'T ANY ANSWER. HOW OFTEN IS THERE ONE?
HE STOPS, HIS HEART STILL BEATING, HIS BLOOD STILL PUMPING.

THEN, AGAINST HIS WILL, HIS HANDS REACH OUT TO TOUCH A NEWLY PLASTERED SECTION OF WALL, AND HIS EYES DART ABOUT AND NOTICE A PICK THROWN CASUALLY ASIDE.
WITHOUT WANTING TO, HE HEFTS THE PICK.

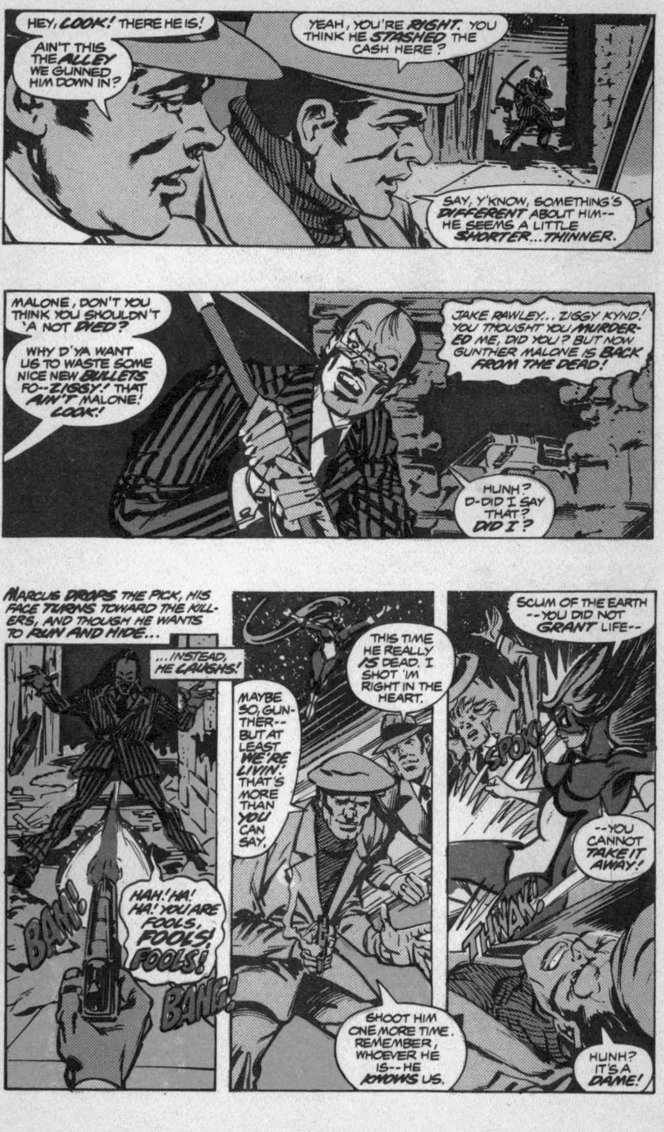

MARCUS DROPS THE PICK, HIS FACE TURNS TOWARD THE KILLERS, AND THOUGH HE WANTS TO RUN AND HIDE...

...INSTEAD, HE LAUGHS!

BAM!

HAH! HA! HA! YOU ARE FOOLS, FOOLS! FOOLS!

BANG!

THIS TIME HE REALLY IS DEAD. I SHOT 'IM RIGHT IN THE HEART.

MAYBE SO, GUNTHER-- BUT AT LEAST WE'RE LIVIN'. THAT'S MORE THAN YOU CAN SAY.

SHOOT HIM ONE MORE TIME. REMEMBER, WHOEVER HE IS--HE KNOWS US.

SCUM OF THE EARTH --YOU DID NOT GRANT LIFE--

SPOK!

--YOU CANNOT TAKE IT AWAY!

THWAK!

HUNH? IT'S A DAME!

YOU CANNOT TAKE THAT WHICH IS NOT YOURS!
THWAK
THOK
THE MONEY YOU STOLE FROM THE CHILDREN'S HOSPITAL... THE MONEY MALONE STOLE FROM YOU-- MUST BE RETURNED!

SPAK!
AND YOU MUST BE PUNISHED FOR YOUR MISDEEDS!

WH-WHO ARE YOU? WHAT'S GOING ON HERE?
WHY DID THOSE MEN SHOOT AT ME? I... I DON'T UNDERSTAND ANY OF THIS.
BULLET HOLES BY YOUR HEART. YET, YOU SURVIVED?
THEY BELIEVED YOU TO BE SOMEONE ELSE... A MAN WHOSE SUIT YOU ARE WEARING.

I-- I DID? HO--
IT MUST BE THE BOOK! LOOK, THEIR BULLETS ARE BURIED IN THE BOOK.
I'M SORRY. I CAN'T BELIEVE THIS... I JUST CAN'T.
WHY DID YOU COME HERE.. DID YOU KNOW OF GUNTHER MALONE?
I DON'T KNOW ANYTHING-- SOMEHOW I WAS FORCED TO COME HERE...FORCED TO CRACK OPEN THAT WALL.

WAIT, DON'T GO! WHAT DO I DO?
NOTIFY THE POLICE. DO YOUR DUTY! I AM SURE THERE IS A REWARD FOR THESE KILLERS... AND FOR THE STOLEN MONEY!
FAREWELL.
B-BUT-- WHO ARE YOU? WHO??
HOME...
I CAN'T EXPLAIN IT, BUT THIS SUIT SEEMS TO BE BEHIND EVERYTHING. IT'S SOMEHOW--CURSED!
CURSED? MARCUS, MY LOVE--IT GOT YOU A JOB... A REWARD... AND IT KEPT YOU ALIVE TO BE WITH ME NOW.
IT IS NOT A CURSE... IT'S A BLESSING-- FOR BOTH OF US... A BLESSING...
NEXT ISSUE: THE NEEDLE!